SOAR

SOAR

Tracy Edward Wymer

Aladdin

New York   London   Toronto   Sydney   New Delhi

This book is a work of fiction. Any references to historical events, real people, or real places are used fictitiously. Other names, characters, places, and events are products of the author's imagination, and any resemblance to actual events or places or persons, living or dead, is entirely coincidental.

ALADDIN

An imprint of Simon & Schuster Children's Publishing Division

1230 Avenue of the Americas, New York, New York 10020

First Aladdin paperback edition July 2017

Text copyright © 2016 by Tracy Edward Wymer

Jacket illustration copyright © 2016 by Brian Biggs

Also available in an Aladdin hardcover edition.

All rights reserved, including the right of reproduction in whole or in part in any form.

ALADDIN is a trademark of Simon & Schuster, Inc., and related logo is a registered trademark of Simon & Schuster, Inc.

For information about special discounts for bulk purchases, please contact Simon & Schuster Special Sales at 1-866-506-1949 or business@simonandschuster.com.

The Simon & Schuster Speakers Bureau can bring authors to your live event.

For more information or to book an event, contact the Simon & Schuster Speakers Bureau at 1-866-248-3049 or visit our website at www.simonspeakers.com.

Jacket designed by Karin Paprocki

Interior designed by Mike Rosamilia

The text of this book was set in Avenir.

0617 OFF

2 4 6 8 10 9 7 5 3 1

This book has been cataloged with the Library of Congress.

ISBN 978-1-4814-4711-9 (hc)

ISBN 978-1-4814-4712-6 (pbk)

ISBN 978-1-4814-4713-3 (eBook)

To my parents—
who taught me to fly.

But Hopes are Shy Birds flying at a great distance seldom reached by the best of Guns.

—John James Audubon

Searching
for Gold

I'm looking for a bird, but not just any old bird. I'm looking for Dad's golden eagle. And I'm not stopping until I find it.

Dad said it was the *most magnificent, most spectacular* bird he'd ever seen, and that's saying something, because Dad had seen more birds than John Audubon himself. And if you don't know who John Audubon was, he was like the Beatles of birding. Yeah, he was *that* famous.

This golden eagle's wings were wider than the creek behind our house, and its talons were the size of bulldozer claws. Dad saw the golden eagle swoop down near Miss Dorothy's pond and snatch a rabbit the size of a lawn mower. The most unique thing about the golden eagle was that it had a gray spot on its wing. Dad called it a birthmark. A birthmark! Can you believe birds have birthmarks?

Dad told everyone about the golden eagle, including his friends in his local birding group. He wasn't expecting to see such a spectacular bird, so he didn't have a camera with him. And without a picture, no one believed him.

But Dad stood by his golden eagle story.

After a while his friends said they were sick of his lies and told him to take his stories elsewhere. They even voted him out of their birding group. So much for being "professional" friends.

The rumors got so bad that other birding groups wanted nothing to do with him. They thought the golden eagle (and Dad) was a big joke.

Still, Dad never gave up. We went looking for the golden eagle at least once a month. He said that seeing a bird that magnificent was the ultimate once-in-a-lifetime sighting, but I hadn't used my once-in-a-lifetime card yet, so there was a chance we could see it.

He promised it would eventually come back, and

Soar

I'm going to be here when it happens. But since Dad's no longer here to defend his story, finding that golden eagle and restoring his reputation depends on one person.

Me.

So here I am—just me, my bike, my binoculars, and my backpack—on the very last day of summer vacation, the day before seventh grade begins, looking for that golden eagle at Miss Dorothy's place, which sits at the far end of my neighborhood.

I walk around Miss Dorothy's pond while twigs crunch under my shoes. The late afternoon sun cooks the black water, and the smell of algae and dead fish slaps me in the face. I've been here a thousand times, and the smell is so bad that I still have to cover my nose with my T-shirt. The end of summer is the worst, because on hot and humid days like today, the stench burns your nose hairs and sticks to your clothes.

High up in an oak tree, a house finch lets out a long, complicated warble that ends in a low-pitched slur.

Then a different call—*cak-cak-cak*—overtakes the singsongy chatter and echoes through the trees.

It's Coop.

She was born twelve years ago, the same year as me, which is pretty old for a Cooper's hawk. She wears speckled plumage like a lot of ordinary hawks, but Coop is far from ordinary. First off, she's really old. Second, she only has one eye.

Dad said she lost it to a black vulture in midair. Coop won the fight, because the vulture flew away from Coop's territory and never came back.

Hawks are supposed to have better eyesight than Superman. Their eyes drive the hunt. That's how they eat, how they survive. But somehow Coop has made it this long. Dad always called her a "tough son of a gun," and that's exactly what I'm going to have to be if I want to find that golden eagle.

Looking through my binoculars, I find Coop swooping overhead, searching for her next meal. She's used to hunting with me around, so she won't mind if I watch her do her thing.

She lands quietly on a branch and scopes the ground.

Near the pond something stirs in the tall cattails.

Coop watches.

Waits.

I crouch low in the brush, adjusting the shoulder

straps of my backpack, keeping my binoculars steady. Seeing Coop hunt never gets old.

A rabbit suddenly leaps out from the cattails and races for cover under a pile of branches.

From high above, Coop launches off the tree and dives straight toward the rabbit. She sinks her talons into the rabbit's back and takes off into the sky, but half-way back to her nest she lets go. The rabbit free-falls and splashes into the black pond.

Too heavy.

Sometimes that happens. It's part of nature.

Dad said the food chain is brutal and that most people don't have the emotional detachment to see it in action. To be honest, seeing a living being take its last breath is not something I'm interested in doing again, but I guess it comes with the territory of study-ing birds.

I check my watch and decide I'd better get home for dinner before Mom comes looking for me.

Before I leave Miss Dorothy's place, I search around the pond for traces of the golden eagle's diet. A par-tially eaten rabbit or bird. The tail of a field mouse. Mauled squirrels or chipmunks.

But there's nothing.

I'm hoping the golden eagle will show up closer to winter, during migration season. That's probably my best chance to see it.

"Eddie," Dad told me, "in order to see a bird like the golden eagle, you have to catch it on the move, while it's going from one home to the next. They're very rare here in Indiana, but spotting it during the fall or winter might be our big chance."

So finding it on the move is my plan, and I'm sticking to it.

Before I leave, I sit under a tree. I take my bird journal out of my backpack, flip to a clean page in the Raptors section, and write:

Bird: Golden eagle
Location: Miss Dorothy's place
Note: Increase search time closer to migration
    season.
Dad: Our bird is going to come back, I just know it.
And when it does, everyone will know the truth.

Papa and the New Girl

On my way home from Miss Dorothy's place, I notice a moving truck sitting in the driveway of a house down the street from mine.

I skid to a stop on my bike. The moving truck is supposed to be white, but it's so dirty that it looks like someone gave it a bath in charcoal.

This house used to be the Lathams', but Timmy's dad lost his job, so they moved back to Kentucky. Now someone new is moving in, and since I've lived in this neighborhood my whole life, I feel like it's my responsibility to investigate our new neighbors.

I hop off my bike and set it down carefully in the

ditch. Hiding your bike is the first step in a spy mission. I know this because Dad and me used to watch old spy movies together. Every Saturday night when I wasn't hanging out at Jetz Skating Rink, I watched a ninja or spy save the day, while sharing popcorn with Dad.

If your mode of transportation—in this case my bike—is seen by the subject, then your mission is doomed. Plus, my bike is more than just a way to get around town.

Last year, right before he flew away, Dad bought my bike at Dan's Sporting Goods. I say "flew away" because it's better than saying "he died" or "passed away." I think Dad would want me to say it like that anyway.

Standing in the aisle, I looked at bikes for almost an hour, but Dad never lost his patience. When I told him I wanted the silver Predator, he just nodded quietly. Then, at the counter, he scribbled on a check, ripped it out, and handed it to me and said, "You pay the gal."

I took the check and stared at it. One hundred and forty-nine dollars was the most money I'd ever held in my hands, and at that moment I didn't want to give it up. But I had to, or else I would've had nothing to show for turning twelve.

Soar

That night Dad said the bike was too big for me, but he also said it was a good choice because I could grow into it.

So you see, my bike is way more than *just* a bike.

In the driveway two moving guys unload a couple of boxes from the moving truck. They're big guys, built like bodyguards or pro wrestlers. Once they go inside the house, I creep through the side yard and sneak around back. I try my best to stay low and quiet, out of sight from windows. The last thing I need is my new neighbors catching me snooping around their house.

A privacy fence stretches all the way around the backyard. I'm five-foot-four-and-a-quarter, so by standing next to it, I can tell it's about six feet tall. I need something to stand on, but all I find in the side yard are a couple of toy fire trucks, a rubber snake, and a Donald Duck walkie-talkie set—all stuff the Lathams left behind.

Caw! Caw!

I duck and cover my head.

The call is harsh and loud.

An eastern bluebird perches on a telephone wire, but the call definitely isn't coming from a dinky songbird like that.

Caw! Caw!

It sounds like it's coming from the backyard, behind the privacy fence. I have to find a way to see it.

Trees surround the house, but none have branches low enough to climb. I spot a half-deflated basketball sitting in the grass. It's the same ball Timmy used when he whipped my butt in H-O-R-S-E every day after school.

I drop the ball next to the fence and stand on it. It rolls back and forth under my shoes, so I hold on to the fence for balance. The only way to see into the backyard is to do a forward pull-up, so that's what I do.

The backyard is smaller than I remember. It's empty except for a covered porch and a shed in the far corner. I can only look over the fence for a few seconds at a time, and then I have to lower my feet onto the basketball to rest. The ball squishes under my weight and shifts side to side, so I keep a tight hold on the fence.

The screen door creaks and swings open. I do another forward pull-up to see who's coming out of the house. It's a dark-skinned man—actually, he looks really tan—with black hair and a long black beard.

But the best part is, a giant parrot stands on his shoulder!

Soar

It's the brightest, most colorful bird I've ever seen. Red feathers cover its head and stomach, and the wings are yellow, green, and blue. Its red tail feathers point straight down, and its beak looks as big as my fist.

You only see these kinds of birds in three places: books, jungles, or zoos. Since the closest jungle is in South America—maybe Mexico—and the closest zoo is across the Indiana–Ohio border in Cincinnati, I don't have much experience with parrots. But thanks to the *Encyclopedia of Macaws* in the West Plains Library, which has my name listed on the checkout card three times, I'm sure this bird is a scarlet macaw.

On the covered porch the man unhinges the door to a huge wire cage and sets the macaw inside. The bird hops onto a long, thin bar, where it perches next to another macaw that could be its twin.

My arms begin to tremble, so I lower myself and rest my feet on the basketball. I shake out my hands one at a time to get the feeling back. Then I take a deep breath and do pull-up number three, more than I've ever done in gym class.

The screen door swings open again. This time it's a tan girl with long, dark hair that hangs to her lower back. She looks like she's in high school, but I hope she's in middle school. She doesn't have to be in seventh grade like me, but at least middle school.

The girl says something to the tan man, but "papa" is all I understand. Papa gestures while mouthing a few words, but no sound comes out of his mouth.

My grip weakens. It takes all my strength to keep my eyes above the fence.

I'm about to lower myself onto the basketball again when a shaggy yellow dog sprints around the corner of the house, barking and growling.

The dog pounces toward me and knocks the basketball out from under my feet. I hold on to the fence, my legs dangling beneath me. The dog jumps up and bites at my shirt.

At the same time the two macaws scream:

Caw! Caw!

Papa and the girl turn and see me.

Uh-oh.

My spy mission is over.

I jump down from the fence and take off running, but my foot catches something in the yard, and I trip.

The last thing I remember is thinking *spies don't get caught* before face-planting into a rock.

I'm Called
a Spy

My head is cold. I blink twice and open my eyes.
I'm lying on a couch.

Where am I? How long have I been here?

The tan girl pulls a bag of ice away from the throbbing spot above my right eye. She kneels on the floor in front of me. Straight black hair outlines her face. Her round eyes look like the acorns I sometimes collect at Miss Dorothy's place.

The man she calls Papa stands between the living room and the kitchen, stroking his black beard. One of the scarlet macaws perches on his leather shoulder strap. The bird is massive, and now that I'm closer to it, its colors are even more impressive. It glares at me like it's about to belt out another warning call.

"You tripped over this." The girl holds up the Donald Duck walkie-talkie set I spotted in the side yard.

From the way she talks, she's definitely not Indiana-an. And now that she's right in front of me, she looks fifteen, maybe sixteen.

I sit up on the couch, and the room goes wobbly for a second.

"Does your head have pain?" she asks.

"A little." I wince and feel the bump above my eye. I blink three times, hoping one of the blinks will straighten everything out.

I look around and realize I'm inside the Lathams' old house. I've been in here for a snack and a drink of water, but it looks way different than it used to. Now all the furniture is made of polished wood, and there are brightly colored pillows everywhere. Boxes fill the empty spaces in the room, and a green-and-yellow flag hangs on the far wall. I don't recognize the flag's words. They're not Spanish but some other language.

"I'm Gabriela. This is my father, Papa. Here, drink this." She takes a bowl from the coffee table and offers it to me. Steam rises from the top of it. I'm afraid if I drink this stuff, it'll burn all the way down to my toes.

"What is it?" I try to sound curious, not rude.

"Papa makes it from acai berries. He says it gives you strength."

Papa pets the macaw's head and smiles.

The macaw glares at me. I can tell it wants me to leave.

I take the bowl from Gabriela. The steam smells like grape juice and black licorice. Whatever it is, it can't be that bad. I blow on the purplish liquid, purse my lips, and take the smallest sip ever while trying to keep my mouth from catching fire.

The liquid burns on the way down, but only for a second. Then the burning goes away and a cool sensation spreads through my chest and shoulders. I shiver and smack my lips together. I have to admit, it tastes pretty good, like a combination of Miss Dorothy's blueberry pie, purple Skittles, and Mom's frozen grapes.

"What do you think?" Gabriela asks.

"It's good."

The macaw squawks.

Caw! Caw!

The sound echoes through the house and rattles my brain.

Gabriela's cheeks turn red. "I am sorry," she says.

15

"Silvio can be protective. He makes a good dog watch."

"You mean 'watchdog,'" I say, before I can stop myself.

Gabriela glances down. "Sorry, my English is not that good."

Great, now I've embarrassed her. I try covering my tracks. "No, I'm sorry. Your English is great."

She smiles, and for the first time I realize she has dimples, just like my mom's. "*Obrigada*," she says. "That means 'thank you.'"

I adjust an orange cushion and sit back on the couch. "This place looks totally different from when the Lathams lived here."

"Papa does not know much about decorating, so he leaves it to me."

Papa smiles and continues petting Silvio's head.

I find the green-and-yellow flag again on the far wall. I try to read the words, but I still don't get what it says. "That flag," I say, "where's it from?"

"Brazil," she says.

"You mean, like, Brazil in South America?"

"Yes. It is the only one I know about."

"You moved here all the way from Brazil?"

She looks over her shoulder at Papa and smiles. "We were tired of living there. We wanted to change."

Soar

I say the only thing I can think of: "Change can be good." Dad told me about a time when he said that to Grampa once, but Grampa told him to shut the heck up. Grampa didn't like change very much, so I bet he didn't even say it that nicely. So far, this is going much better.

"I will be in seventh grade," she says. "I am very nervous, but Papa says he will be with me in spirit."

"Seventh grade? Me too!" I can hardly contain my excitement. "You have nothing to be nervous about. West Plains is a good place to live."

She smiles. But I wonder if she's smiling because we're in the same grade, or because she could care less that we're in the same grade but she doesn't want to hurt my feelings.

"That is good," she says. "You can show me the school and answer all of my questions."

I take another sip of Papa's special drink made from berries. Something about this drink really does make you feel better. "Thanks for taking care of me," I say. I turn to the window and notice the orange and blue in the sky meshing together like the plumage of that eastern bluebird. "I should get home before dark."

Gabriela hands me the bag of ice. "Press the ice on

the bump so it does not grow. But do not fall asleep with the ice on your head, or you will wake up with a head pain."

I'm sure she means "headache," but I don't say anything about it. Instead I hold the ice on my head and say, "Okay, thanks."

On my way out I walk past Papa. He flashes a wide smile while scratching his beard. He's thin, with square shoulders and long arms. He taps me on the shoulder and signs something to me, still smiling.

"Papa is deaf and mute," Gabriela says. "He says it was nice to meet you."

I stand at the front door. "Tell him I said it was nice meeting him and Silvio, even if Silvio wants to eat me for dinner."

Gabriela laughs. This time I can tell that her dimples are bigger than Mom's. "Before you leave," she says, "I have one question for you."

I shrug. "Sure, go ahead."

"What is your name?" she asks.

"Oh, right. Sorry about that. I should've introduced myself. I'm Eddie. I live down the street."

I hold out my hand to shake hands, but she crosses her arms.

"Eddie Who Lives Down the Street. Do you always watch your neighbors?"

"You said *one* question, not *two*."

"I am only joking," she says. "You are curious and you want to make sure we are good neighbors. I understand, Eddie."

"I figured you were joking," I tell her.

I'm glad Gabriela has a sense of humor. She lives down the street from me, so there's a good chance I'll see her a lot. Dad and Mom used to laugh all the time, and right now I could use more laughing in my life.

I say good-bye and walk out the door, carrying the bag of ice.

In the driveway the moving guys are still unloading boxes from the truck. One of them pauses from picking up a box and looks at me.

"You okay, kid?" he asks.

"Yeah. I'm fine." I walk toward the ditch, feeling good after Papa's berry drink and my talk with Gabriela.

But when I get to the ditch, it's empty.

My bike is gone.

Mom—
The Janitor

While walking home, I start to panic on the inside. I sort through all the people who might've stolen my bike. The list is short, and I already have a top suspect in mind.

I pick up a rock and aim at the trunk of a sycamore tree. I imagine the top suspect's face pinned to the bark and throw the rock as hard as I can.

But the rock completely misses the tree.

When I get home and walk in the front door, Mom is folding laundry in the living room and watching TV. Her eyes are watery. She's watching one of those talk shows where everyone sits in a half circle and a special guest doctor tries to fix a broken family, all while the audience watches like it's a weirdo circus act. Mom cries when she watches these shows. Seeing all those broken families sitting onstage must remind her of our family and life without Dad.

Mom switches the channel to *One Last Life*, her favorite soap opera, and turns to me, the keys on her belt loop jingling. Mom is the head janitor at my school, so she has about fifty keys attached to her belt loop all the time. I'm okay with her working at my school. She's been taking care of that place since before I was born.

"I told you to be home by dark, Eddie," she says. "Where were you?"

"I was at Miss Dorothy's place."

"The whole time?"

"Well, not the *whole* time."

I tell her about meeting Gabriela from Brazil and having Papa's special berry drink and how it tasted like a mixture of her frozen grapes and Miss Dorothy's blueberry pie.

"What happened to your eye?" she asks, walking closer to me.

"I swerved on my bike and hit my head on a tree branch."

"Eddie, that doesn't look good. I'm getting you some ice." She walks into the kitchen to get an ice pack for me.

Lying makes my stomach wad up tight, but if Mom knew I was spying on our new neighbors she'd lecture me to death. She'd tell me it's rude and then say how disappointed she is. I also don't tell her about my bike being gone. That would mean a double lecture and a triple grounding.

I follow her into the kitchen, open the refrigerator, reach past the milk jug, and take out the orange juice carton. There's only one swig left.

Mom stands at the kitchen sink. She puffs on a cigarette and blows two smoke streams from her nose. I hate Mom's bad habit. She quit cold turkey once. But after the doctor gave us the news about Dad, she started up again. She said it was too much stress, and that she needed something to take away everything that was happening. I told her that tracking birds was healthier and more fun, but she wasn't interested.

I roll my eyes, without her seeing me.

"Here's your ice pack," she says, handing the ice pack to me. "Put it on your bump for ten minutes. It'll help with the swelling. Oh, and I stopped by the Freeze Queen. Burgers are on the table."

Soar

I take a red plastic cup from the cabinet. I pour the last gulp of orange juice into the cup, and I slam it back in one gulp.

"How old is the new girl?" Mom asks.

I pitch the empty orange juice carton into the trash. "I don't know. Thirteen, maybe."

I rummage through the greasy sack on the counter and pull out a Buck Burger. That's right, these burgers are only a dollar. Mom says it's a deal you can't pass up. I unwrap the burger and rip off a bite. "Can you open the window, please?"

Mom raises the window above the sink, her keys clinking together like wind chimes. She takes another puff from her cigarette. "Well, does she seem like a nice girl?"

"Yeah," I say. "She seems nice."

"Don't act so excited, Eddie." She blows smoke out the window while laughing at herself. Her laugh makes her cough the same phlegmy cough Dad used to have, only Dad's cough was from stomach cancer, not from puffing on a cigarette. "Maybe you two can become friends, especially if she lives down the street."

I shrug. "Yeah, maybe."

Mom holds her cigarette out the window, flicks off

the ashes, and looks at me. "Eddie," she says. "You're gonna have to move on at some point. Camilla's not coming back."

The words hurt me inside, but I know they're true. "You're right," I say, and smile at her. She messes up my hair and kisses my forehead.

"Big birthday coming up soon," she says. "What does a soon-to-be-thirteen-year-old boy want these days?"

"Oh, I don't know. New binoculars? Another bird journal?"

"Of course." She rolls her eyes. "Go rest up. You got school tomorrow."

I walk into my room with my wrapped-up dinner. If I could have anything I wanted for my birthday, it would be to have my dad back. But that's not happening, unless it wasn't really him lying in that casket that I watched get lowered six feet underground.

I plop down onto my bed and think about Switzerland and Camilla Caflisch. She was a foreign exchange student from Switzerland. She came to West Plains in fourth grade. Everyone called her Catfish because her last name sounds like it and she has a tiny mouth like a fish.

Soar

Mrs. Rollins introduced Camilla to the class and then assigned me as her pal for the day. Camilla was more interesting than any of the other girls. For one thing, she had a cool accent. She also invited me over for dinner one night, and we had potatoes and cheese and no meat. No meat! Can you believe that? I told her I'd never had a dinner like that before. Mom always has meat on the table, even if it's wrapped up in a greasy sack. When Camilla laughed at my joke, her mouth didn't look like a fish mouth. It looked more like a Carolina chickadee's beak.

Camilla and I were best friends. We did everything together. She introduced me to tennis, which I still can't play, and I introduced her to birds.

At the end of fourth grade, Camilla went back to Switzerland. We wrote messages to each other all summer long. She told me about the Swiss Alps, and how she was doing a lot of hiking. She also said her family might move to Hong Kong because of her dad's job. I told her everything would be okay and that she was cool enough to make friends anywhere. After that I didn't hear from her again. I'm pretty sure they have email in Hong Kong. Maybe her dad didn't like that she was writing to a boy all the time.

The only bad part about being assigned Camilla's pal for the day was the name everyone started calling me. Fish Boy. The kid who made it up is the same kid who's the top suspect for stealing my bike.

His real name is Raymond, but he goes by his middle name—MOUTON.

"Mouton" rhymes with what a cow does—MOO—and what time I wake up to go birding—DAWN.

MOO—TAWN.

I didn't see Mouton take my bike. But since he's an overgrown ogre who lives in my neighborhood and we've hated each other since kindergarten, there's a good chance it was him.

I'm not letting him get away with stealing my wheels. I'll get my bike back if it takes me all year to do it.

I'll bet a hundred and forty-nine dollars on it.

Dad—
The Birder

One night two years ago, Dad and I were eating Buck Burgers at the Freeze Queen. Mom was working late at school, so it was just the two of us.

Dad didn't look so good. He was pale, and sweat was beading on his forehead. He put his burger down, coughed twice, and took off to the bathroom. He didn't even say "excuse me" like he normally did. He just zipped away, holding napkins over his mouth.

When he came back, his eyes were wet, and tiny red dots covered his face. Normally Dad was a handsome guy. I wouldn't know, but that's what I overheard Mrs. Rollins say to the teacher's aide who helped out on

Tuesdays and Thursdays. Right then Dad wasn't in the same bird sanctuary as handsome.

A lady who worked at the Freeze Queen came up to our table and said, "Mr. Wilson, are you okay?"

Dad dabbed his eyes with a napkin and said, "I'm fine. Can we have one banana split with two spoons, please?"

She looked concerned for Dad, but she said "You got it" and walked away.

The next day, when I asked Dad to go on a bike ride, he was too tired. When I asked him to hang the new hummingbird feeder, his arms were too sore. The next weekend, I showed up in the living room with my binoculars slung over my shoulder and asked him to go look for the golden eagle. For the first time, he said no. "Sorry, Eddie, I don't think I can do it today."

He turned away from me, but not before I caught his expression. Pain, fear, sadness all rolled up into one.

He never said no to birding. That was his life.

One day I finally asked, "Dad, are you going to be okay?"

"Yes, Eddie," he said. "Okay as a blue jay."

Dad wasn't a bird-watcher. He was a birder. There's a big difference, and he made sure I knew about it.

Soar

"If you can't hear 'em, you're only a watcher," he told me. "A real birder sees, hears, feels, and tastes. You have to respect every part of the species, or it won't respect you back."

Dad taught me everything about birding. One night I scooted real close to him on the couch while watching a spy movie.

"Dad, I want to be the best birder in the whole world," I said. "How do I do that?"

He stopped the movie and turned to me. I knew this was going to be a long answer. But that was what I wanted.

He rested his hand on my shoulder. "If you want to be the best, Son, then you have to be creative. You have to think like a bird. You have to *become* the bird."

"*Become* the bird," I said. "What does that mean?"

"You have to ask yourself, if you were that bird, and you were trying to survive, what would you need at that exact moment? Not two days from now, not one week from now, not a year. Ask yourself what that bird needs at that very instant. Food? Protection? Nesting materials? Companionship?"

"What's 'companionship'?" I asked.

Dad smirked and said, "It's about filling a big, empty hole inside you with feelings for someone else."

"You mean like you and mom?"

He smiled and said, "Exactly."

Dad also taught me the Rules of Birding (he called it the Wilson Way):

1. Get as close as you can.
2. Never take your eyes off it.
3. No one gets in your way.

Dad actually made his living as a park ranger, but he took birding seriously and treated it like his second job.

He also loved to tell stories, and sometimes he would exaggerate. One time he told me about a deer jumping over him and his friend while they were riding a scooter. Every time he told the story, the deer grew bigger by two feet!

Up until the time when Dad saw the golden eagle, there had never been one spotted officially in West Plains. According to birding experts, they only visit Indiana in the winter. Dad said he saw the golden eagle in late October, and that's when he thought it would come back. I'm going to be there when it happens.

* * *

Soar

I spend a lot of time with birds. When I'm not at school or at home, you can usually find me at Miss Dorothy's place. That might explain why I don't have many friends.

After Camilla went back to Switzerland, I didn't want to start making friends again, only to be forgotten. Then about a year later, Dad got sick, and well, everyone at school pretty much avoided me after that. Maybe they didn't know how to act around me, or what to say to me. I don't blame them. It's hard seeing people suffer.

In a lot of ways, birds are like people. Everyone thinks they just fly around, chirp, and poop on bikes and cars. But they're more unique than that. They're like having a whole group of friends with different personalities. Some birds are outgoing and aggressive, like the northern mockingbird, while others are quiet and shy, like the whispery mourning dove.

But birds are also different from humans.

For one, birds always stick by your side. They never go away, like people do. Sure, they might fly away for a short time, but they'll eventually come back. Go outside and look up. You'll see or hear at least one or two birds. If you don't, just wait thirty seconds. I bet you won't be disappointed.

Raptors are the best, the birds with sharp eyes and beaks.

One time when I was in fifth grade, I saw a red-tailed hawk swoop down and pick up a squirrel. It took off to the sky and never came back. I'm sure the red-tailed fed its family and was only trying to survive in the wild, but I couldn't help but feel sorry for the squirrel. Dad could tell that it bothered me, so that night he explained the food chain to me.

"Here's how it works, Eddie. At the top of the triangle we have humans, like me and you and your mom. Below us are sharks and crocodiles, animals who can kill almost anything but don't benefit from having an intelligent brain like you and me. Then come the other species, and one of those species is birds. Now, birds are special creatures. For one, they fly. Two, they have feathers. Three, they're better-looking than anything else on earth, besides you, your mom, and deer."

That last part he said while pointing his finger at me, like Papa pointing his finger at Silvio for squawking at me so rudely.

"It's a tough world out there, Son, but birds always find a way to adapt and survive. Just imagine what it would be like to fly. Picture that in your mind for a second."

Dad closed his eyes. So I did the same. It was like we were having a moment of silence for birds' ability to fly. But I didn't picture myself flying. I pictured Mom standing next to a deer.

"What about an ostrich?" I finally said. "It's a bird, and it can't fly."

Dad laughed. "Ostrich? That's not a bird. That's a giraffe that never evolved." He patted my back and mumbled, "Ostrich. You sure keep me on my toes, Eddie."

Dad chuckled at himself and started coughing. He hacked, deep and hard. Then he covered his mouth, and two streams of blood oozed out from between his fingers. It wasn't the light red blood that comes out when you nick your finger while cutting out science flash cards. This was dark blood. The kind bad guys spit up in spy movies when saying their last words.

Dad took off to the bathroom and shut the door. He coughed for a while, and then the toilet flushed.

I sat there on the couch and pulled my legs up to my chest. I held on to my knees, wondering if Dad was right about him being okay.

* * *

At my desk in my bedroom, I open my journal and flip through the birds I've seen this year. I've split them into three categories.

Commons: finches, robins, sparrows, juncos. (These birds are everywhere.)

Betters: orioles, jays, cardinals, hummingbirds. (More interesting than Commons.)

Then there's the best category of all: Raptors. (Unfortunately, some eat Commons and Betters.)

So far this year I've only seen three raptors: Coop, an eastern screech owl, and a sharp-shinned hawk. Coop doesn't really count, because she nests in a giant oak in the woods behind Miss Dorothy's house. Last year I saw a barred owl, and the year before that I saw a red-tailed hawk and an American kestrel.

But no golden eagle.

Never a golden eagle.

I turn to a blank page in the back of my journal and make a new category: Rare Species.

I close my eyes and visualize the scarlet macaw from Gabriela's house. I take a pencil, roll it between my hands, and begin drawing the macaw's head. I always start with the head. It makes it easier to keep the other parts proportionate. There's nothing worse than drawing a bird with an undersize head, oversize beak, and different-size feet. When I first started keeping a bird journal, which was in first grade, I drew an American goldfinch that looked like a miniature version of Big Bird.

The macaw's head and body come out accurate. I add the feet—two toes pointing forward and two pointing backward—and then I draw the massive beak.

I rummage through the colored-pencil box in my desk and find the brightest red, blue, green, and yellow pencils I can find. I begin coloring the body feathers red, and then I color the wing feathers blue and yellow, with a touch of green between them.

Below the macaw I write:

Bird: Scarlet macaw (Silvio)
Location: Gabriela's House
Note: Silvio is the most impressive bird I've ever
    seen up close.
Dad: You should've seen this scarlet macaw! You
    would've loved it.
I have a question for you.
Do you think I'll ever have another best friend?

Honey
Strikes Twice

The first day of school is usually a drag, but I have a feeling seventh grade will be different.

To start with, I'm going to find out who stole my bike.

That next morning I stroll toward the bus stop, as Mom drives by and honks. "See you at school, honey," she says, blowing smoke out the window.

I take the bus in the morning because my parents always wanted me to experience school like a normal kid, like someone whose mom isn't the head janitor there. Mom seems okay with me taking the bus, since she gets to take me home every day.

Soar

We've owned Mom's car since before I was born. I call it Hoopty, because it's basically a piece of junk on wheels. It's an old Impala with rusted side panels, and brakes that squeak loud enough for the whole town to hear. If it weren't in such bad condition, it would be a cool ride. Mom paid Sandy, my bus driver, a dollar for the car. One dollar! Hamburgers cost a dollar, not cars. Sandy told my dad it was to avoid paying some sort of tax and—in his words—giving the government more than they deserve.

Now Mom refuses to part with Hoopty. It has over two hundred thousand miles on it, the radio only works with a coat hanger attached to where the antenna's supposed to go, and the muffler belches black smoke. Mom always tells me "Hoopty" isn't a word. I tell her it's in the urban dictionary, and it's a word that means "a beat-up car." Then she says the urban dictionary is not a real dictionary. I can't win with her sometimes.

A couple of high school kids laugh when Mom drives away. They ride the bus with us because the high school is right next to the middle school. I want to tell them to get lost, but they're a lot bigger than me.

Gabriela stands alone, wearing a red dress.

Then I see him.

Mouton.

MOO-TAWN.

The Biggest, Most Annoying Kid Who Ever Lived.

His hair is sticking up in all directions and looks like a bad case of bed head. He's wearing an oversize white T-shirt and camouflage cargo shorts with strings dangling from the bottom. One of his black high-top shoes is untied.

"Your mom is a loser," he says to me, leaning against the stop sign. He spits, and a wet streak splats onto the pavement. He's as tall as Dad was, but he's a lot wider and shaped like a pear.

Mouton and I are like verbs. We have a past, present, and future. Mom says when we were little, we played together at the park in the sandbox, but then we started kindergarten, and for some reason, everything changed.

Here are some examples of our past:

In first grade Mouton sat on me during recess. In second grade he dumped his science project volcano lava onto my desk and ruined my Cooper's hawk drawing. In third grade he stole my shoes and hid them under the teacher's desk. In fourth grade he started calling me Fish Boy (because of Camilla), and so did everyone else. In fifth grade he locked me in the equipment room, and I was stuck in there for the last two periods of the day.

But last year, in sixth grade, the weirdest thing happened. He didn't do anything. Maybe he was too busy ruining someone else's life.

So it's obvious that we just can't get along, mostly because he's always picking fights with me and being an annoying ogre.

As far as our future together, well, I hope he's not part of mine.

There's something else to know about Mouton. He has Tourette's syndrome, a brain disorder that makes him blurt out words, even if it's at inappropriate times. The worst part is when he gets stuck on a word or phrase and then repeats it until you can't take it anymore. My mom says they're called vocal tics. Mouton has the same one all the time (Yip!), which gets worse when he's nervous. I know I'm supposed to ignore his outbursts, but it's hard to do that when he makes my life miserable on purpose.

I decide to stay where I'm standing, and keep my distance from Mouton. "Leave my mom out of it," I say.

"Sure thing, Big Bird," he says.

"Did you steal my bike?" I ask him.

"What bike?" he says. He picks a pebble up off the street and throws it at my cheek.

"Ouch." I rub my cheek to make the stinging go away.

"What's wrong?" he says. "Got a little boo-boo? Maybe mommy can help you when you get to school. Or maybe she's too busy cleaning toilets."

I ignore Mouton. Sometimes it's the only way to handle him. Up until third grade I gave it right back to him, but now he's three times my size.

Gabriela looks at me, like she's waiting for my response to Mouton. If only I could explain to her that he comes with special handling instructions, and if you're not careful, he'll explode and stomp on buildings like Godzilla.

Bus number thirteen squeals to a stop, black smoke spiraling from the tailpipe. The door opens.

Mouton shoves me aside and cuts in front of everyone.

Gabriela steps back from the crowd, letting others get on the bus in front of her. I hang back a little too, until we're the only ones left standing outside the bus.

Mouton sticks his head out the back window and yells, "Eddie-shovel-truck! Eddie-shovel-truck!"

He's been saying that for two years now, and no one knows why. I think it's because he wants to dump me into a trash truck and then bury me with a shovel.

I turn to Gabriela and say, "He's a jerk. Just ignore him."

"What is a jerk?" she asks.

I could go many places with this one, most of them dark and ugly, but instead I say, "Someone who acts like Mouton."

"The jerk is named Mouton?"

"'Ogre' is what I call him. It means 'a big, clumsy monster.'"

"Oh," she says.

"Can you believe his parents named him Mouton? What were they thinking?"

"The name Mouton is interesting," she says. "I like it better than 'Eddie.'"

I can't decide whether to be embarrassed or mad or both. So what do I do? I say the dumbest thing ever said in The History of Responses to Girls:

"Yeah, you're right. My name *is* stupid."

Sandy, the bus driver, whistles. "Come on, love-birds. I've got a schedule to keep," he says, waving us up the steps.

I walk up the first two steps, and Sandy looks up at

me from underneath his gray hat, which is round in the front and flat on top. "Good to see you, Eddie."

I smile at Sandy and say, "Good to see you, too."

I drift down the aisle and stop short of the back row. Mouton lies down and stretches out across two seats. He sleeps every morning on the way to school. Most days he ends up snoring by the time we pull into the parking lot. I always think about getting revenge while he's sleeping—taking his backpack and hiding it—but then I chicken out and end up looking out the window.

I sling my backpack into a seat and fall in next to it.

Gabriela sets her bag down and eases into the seat across the aisle. She reaches into her bag, pulls out an orange notebook, and places it next to her. The notebook matches the orange design on her red dress, like it's part of her special first-day-of-school outfit.

Gabriela clicks her pen, opens to the first page, and begins writing.

"What's with the notebook?" I ask her.

She ignores me.

I try again. "What's with the—"

"I hear you," she says. "The notebook is a gift from Papa. It is to write down important words so I can learn better English."

"Sorry," I say. "I didn't mean to pry."

"'Pry'? What does this mean?"

"It means 'to stick your nose in someone's business.'"

"'Pry.' I will write that one down. Thank you, Eddie."

She begins writing it in her notebook, so I spell it for her. "*P-R-Y.*" She looks up and smiles, this time a full smile, like she's suddenly comfortable around me.

"How is the bump on your head?" she asks me.

"It's getting better. The swelling went down." I point it out, showing her where the bump used to be. "See?"

"Yes, I see." She closes her notebook.

"Thanks for the bag of ice. I think it helped a lot."

"You are welcome, Eddie. You are—how do you say it?—very sweet."

She giggles, covering her smile. Her cheeks turn pink.

I take in a deep breath. The clothes I'm wearing— stained khaki shorts, Dad's faded Black Crowes T-shirt, and sneakers with holes in them—suddenly feel like a brand-new first-day-of-school outfit, just like Gabriela's.

Maybe there's hope for our friendship, after all.

Gabriela goes back to writing in her notebook.

I stare out the window, looking for cardinals and hawks and golden eagles. I don't see any of those, but I hear a downy woodpecker in a tree. No one else is listening closely enough to hear it, so I just sit back and smile while letting the morning breeze hit my face.

Finally the bus pulls into the school parking lot.

Mouton wakes up and elbows his way to the front, saying he has to see the principal about his schedule.

Gabriela tucks her notebook into her bag and starts down the aisle. I follow close behind, hoping she asks for help finding her locker or homeroom. Who better to ask than me? I've got experience in helping students from other countries.

As we get to the front, Sandy sticks out his arm and stops me. "Eddie," he says. "Can I talk to you for a minute?"

"Sure," I say, stopping to listen.

Gabriela walks down the steps without me, without her "pal" for the day, and she doesn't even look back to say "bye." What will she do without me? How will she find her way around? Who will tell her what words like "pry" mean?

Sandy pokes his hat with his finger and it tilts up on his head. "How's your mom doing?" he asks.

"Okay." I keep my response short.

Gabriela is already out of sight. I'll never see her again, because she'll be whisked away by the popular girls, and the popular girls don't ever talk to me.

"You sure about that?" Sandy asks.

"Yeah, I'm sure."

"Okay. But remember, I'm here if you two need anything. I mean it. I'm right here, in the driver's seat."

"Thanks, Sandy. I know where to find you."

Sandy grins. He's not fully toothless, but he's missing two teeth in his smile.

Dad and Sandy were good friends. They talked a lot about birds, and Dad always brought Sandy leftovers from dinner. But Sandy didn't show up at Dad's funeral. Mom said it was wrong of Sandy to stand Dad up like that, so she hasn't talked to him since then.

I jump down the bus steps and walk toward school.

There's no chance of finding Gabriela in the first day chaos, so instead I search for my locker in the seventh-grade hallway. I rummage in my bag for a slip of paper with my locker combo scribbled on it. I give the lock a couple of turns and pull up on the handle.

Right away something smells funny.

Not funny, but sweet.

It's actually a nice smell, like Mom came by and de-germed my locker. It wouldn't surprise me if she had. Mom does a lot of awesome things like that. Last year, on the first day of sixth grade, I opened my locker and found a note with a folded-up twenty-dollar bill in it. Mom said that it was my reward for making it to middle school.

Thinking nothing else of the smell, I take my books, pencil, and bird journal out of my backpack and throw my backpack into the locker. My bag lands in a lump of translucent brown goo.

I walk closer to the locker, stick my head inside, and smell.

It's honey.

I pull my backpack from the locker, but it's too late. The bottom of it is caked in stickiness.

"Problem, honey?"

It's him again.

Mouton.

MOO-TAWN.

He's leaning against his locker on the other side of the hallway.

"'Look out, look out. I need to talk to the principal about my schedule.' You really bought that bag of smoke, didn't you, Bird Boy?"

I wipe my hands across my shorts, but that only spreads the honey and makes everything twice as sticky.

I throw my backpack down and take off toward the bathroom.

Soar

Grabbing the bathroom door handle, I slam face-first into a sheet of red, otherwise known as Gabriela's dress.

"Eddie?" she says. "This is the *girls'* bathroom."

"Oh, sorry," I say.

I turn around and hurry away, my face and neck and every other part of me becoming hot and tingly.

"Eddie," Gabriela calls after me. "What is wrong?"

"Mouton!" I say, without turning around.

Great. The first day of seventh grade is going just how I imagined it.

Not.

Blue-Ribbon Redemption

I've been in science class for twenty minutes, and my dad was right, Mr. Dover is full of hot air. First off, he wears a navy-blue bow tie. Everyone knows that only people who think they're really smart wear bow ties. The only good part about his bow tie is that it's covered with little white ducks.

Mr. Dover began class by talking about rocks and minerals, and then he started talking about a rock he found at his house, and the next thing you know he's telling a story about an owl plucking a rodent from his property. I don't mind stories about birds. I mean, owls are silent assassins and ninja-like hunters, so I can see why Mr. Dover talks about them. But every other sentence out of Mr. Dover's mouth has to be about *his* property.

Mr. Dover rolls up his sleeves and takes a green marker from the white-board tray. He writes "SCIENCE SYMPOSIUM" in capital letters on the white board.

"West Plains has a reputation for producing world-class scientists," he says. "Seventh graders, just like you, who have gone on to become leading experts in their fields. You have a chance to become one of them when you display your project at our annual event, the Seventh-Grade Science Symposium."

Last year, when I was in sixth grade, the whole grade was invited to tour the symposium during the last fifteen minutes, once the parents and judges had seen all the projects.

If you ask me, the projects were pretty average.

There were the usual inventions: automatic dog food dispenser, high-tech garden-watering system, and lap desk with lights and drink holders. One kid actually tried to create a real homework machine that only did math. The homework machine would've been cool, but every answer came out wrong.

There were also creative projects: blindfolded

roller-skating dogs, pickle jar binoculars, and diet candy that makes you lose weight.

Then there were the real contenders: sheep and their abnormal family structure, microwavable shape-shifting Play-Doh, the social networking agenda of flowers, and the winner—professional sports and its influence on the lightning bug's life cycle.

There was only one project about birds, but it was sloppily thrown together—probably the night before. It compared the red-bellied woodpecker with the red-headed woodpecker, which is the most ridiculous and most obvious bird project ever done, if you could really call it a project.

When my dad was in seventh grade, he won the blue ribbon. His symposium project proved that the number of sharp-shinned hawks in a given territory negatively correlates to the number of songbirds. Basically, the more sharp-shinned hawks, the fewer songbirds, because the hawks eat them all.

If I can just find that golden eagle, and win the blue ribbon—like Dad—then maybe everyone will believe Dad actually saw it—that he really *was* telling the truth.

Mr. Dover caps the green marker, and the classroom

door opens. Standing there is Mrs. Hughes, with her arm around Gabriela!

I smile big and wave at her. She smiles back, but doesn't wave.

"Mr. Dover," Mrs. Hughes says, "this is our newest seventh grader, Gabriela."

Mr. Dover steps forward, drumming the green marker in his hand. "Thank you, Mrs. Hughes."

Mrs. Hughes pats Gabriela on the arm and walks out, closing the door behind her.

"Gabriela," Mr. Dover says, "we were just discussing the science symposium."

"I have been told it is a big event," she says.

"You hear that, folks? Even our newest student knows about the symposium."

Gabriela smiles, her cheeks turning pink.

"But for now," Mr. Dover says, "we're going to move on to our first unit. For the first few weeks we'll be studying birds."

My heart flutters and flaps its wings. I want to stand up and shout "Yes!" so the entire school can hear me. But instead I rest my hand on top of my bird journal, which is sitting on top of my science book.

"I hate birds," Mouton says.

I glare at Mouton, my eyes telling him to *BE QUIET!*

Mr. Dover ignores him and keeps talking. "A bird-watcher is a special kind of person. Most of the time they live a solitary life, one that revolves around their subjects. It takes patience, commitment, and compassion to understand the full existence of a bird."

I feel like Mr. Dover wrote this lesson for me!

Mr. Dover straightens his bow tie, and the little white ducks move (fly) up and down. "Does anyone know the three rules to bird-watching?" he asks.

I shoot my hand into the air. So does Mouton.

I'm pretty sure that Mouton doesn't know the difference between a canary and a crow. He definitely doesn't know the Rules of Birding.

Mr. Dover calls on me. "Eddie, go ahead and tell us."

"I prefer the term 'birding', not 'bird-watching.' 'Birding' includes everything: adaptations, calls, nesting and feeding habits, migration patterns, mating, not just *watching* birds."

"That's great, Eddie," Mr. Dover says. "But do you know the answer to the question?"

Everyone turns to me, including Gabriela. She's probably thinking I'm way out of my league here.

I've known these rules since I could talk. Every time

Soar

I went out with Dad, he'd say them at the beginning of our trip, and then he'd make me repeat them at the end.

"That's easy," I say. "Get as close as you can to the bird. Never take your eyes off it. Don't let anyone get in your way."

Everyone laughs, but I don't know what's so funny.

"That's quite a list, Eddie," Mr. Dover says. "But whoever told you these rules has unfortunately misled you. The first rule of birding is to stay at a comfortable distance, so you don't scare the bird. Rule number two is to only look at the bird long enough to make your observations before writing them in your journal. Every birder knows that if you stare at one bird for too long, then you may miss another bird flying your way. The third rule is the exact opposite of what you said. You should strive to be courteous to others in the field. You never know when you might need a helping hand from a fellow birder."

"Take that," Mouton says. He leans back in his chair while tapping his pen on his desk.

"Eddie," Mr. Dover says, "the rules of birding have been around longer than trees. A real birder would not only know these rules by heart, but he would live by them every day. Where did you learn about these rules?"

"From my dad," I say.

"Hmm," he says.

"My dad also said that a real birder would never put red food coloring in hummingbird feeders, like you do, because two recent studies have shown it could be harmful."

I've never talked like this to a teacher before. I don't know why I'm saying these things. It's like I can't control myself. I don't know whether to be embarrassed, proud, or scared for my science grade.

Mouton's chair drops to the floor. "Bird Nerd, Bird Nerd, Bird Nerd," he says. Then he makes the same weird sound he always makes when he's nervous. "Yip!"

Mr. Dover glances at the clock hanging on the back wall above the bulletin board. On the clock common backyard birds fill the spaces where numbers usually go. "Time's up. Eddie," he says, "I'd like to speak to you after class."

Everyone picks up their books and walks out. I hope for a glance from Gabriela—just one glance—but she offers nothing.

So much for being best friends.

Mouton walks by and says, "Eddie-shovel-truck! Yip!"

Once everyone has left the classroom, I gather my

books, with my bird journal resting on top, and walk to the front of the room. I'm sure this conversation is going to be short. It will probably end with me sitting outside Mrs. Hughes's office.

How am I going to explain to Mom that I got sent to the principal's office on the first day of school?

I don't waste any time. "I'm really sorry, Mr. Dover. I didn't mean what I said. It just sort of slipped out. I won't do it again."

Mr. Dover says, "Eddie, I want to show you something."

He walks behind the front table and puts on a leather falconry glove. He bends down and fiddles with what sounds like a metal cage. He stands up, holding a bird on his gloved hand.

The bird is striking. It has a blue head and wings, and a rusty-red back and tail, and black specks cover its body. Its beak is small and points sharply downward, exactly like Coop's. It's a good-size bird, smaller than a peregrine falcon but bigger than a red-winged blackbird.

"That's a male American kestrel," I say. "The smallest falcon in North America."

"Very good, Eddie. Say hi to Zeus."

"Hi, Zeus," I say.

As much as I like birds, I've never actually talked to one. It feels as weird as it sounds.

"I found him hobbling around on my property. He was in a tree that was struck by lightning. He has a broken wing. It's healing, but gradually. Go ahead, you can touch his head."

The bird stares at me. I stroke his head, and he looks up toward the ceiling. My other hand rests on my bird journal. What I wouldn't do to take my journal out right now and compare one of my American kestrel sketches to Zeus.

Mr. Dover strokes Zeus's nape, the back of his neck.

"Eddie," he says, "your father was his own man. He did things his own way. I'm not saying that's a bad thing, but not everyone always agreed with his way."

"Did you agree with his way?" I ask.

"Not very often."

"Why not?"

"Look, Eddie. The most important thing is that you and I have one thing in common, a very important thing. We both love birds. We can agree to disagree on the Rules of Birding, I'm fine with that. But we have a long year ahead of us in science, so let's start over. What do you say?"

Soar

The bird clock chirps. The hour hand rests on an American goldfinch, which means it's ten o'clock.

With his free hand Mr. Dover scribbles on a notepad and rips off the top sheet. "Here's a pass. You have five minutes to get to your next class."

I take the pass and walk toward the classroom door.

"Hey," Mr. Dover says. "Zeus likes you. I can tell."

I give a half smile and walk out of the room.

I'm sure Mr. Dover says this to every student who shows any signs of trouble, especially those who point out his poor birding methods in front of the whole class.

The way Zeus looks at me is kind of weird, though. It's like he knows me already, or we've met before.

I wonder if that's how the golden eagle would look at me.

During lunchtime in the cafeteria, while sitting alone, I open my bird journal to a clean page in the Raptors section and begin drawing Zeus. I sketch the head and the small, sharp beak, including the black vertical lines on both sides of his face. Then I draw the slate-blue wings, with brown spots, and the rust-colored back and tail.

The American kestrel is about the size of a mourning

dove, so the drawing doesn't take that long. Below the drawing I write:

> Bird: American Kestrel (Zeus)
> Location: Mr. Dover's classroom
> Note: Zeus's wing is healing; I hope he flies again.
> Dad: Do you think Mr. Dover doesn't like me because of something that happened between you and him?
> I wish you were here to tell me more.
> I wish . . . I wish . . . I wish . . .

Feathered
Psycho

After math class I talk to Mrs. Hughes and she gives me a new locker next to Trixie Longburger's. Trixie has bright orange hair and matching braces. She's always chewing gum, and she talks faster than anyone else in school.

We have an ongoing conversation between classes, which is only five minutes, so by the time I walk to my locker (while avoiding Mouton), open it, and get books for my next class, I'd say our conversation takes place over a total of forty-five seconds.

Conversation with Trixie—Part I

Trixie: What are you doing here?

Me: Mrs. Hughes moved my locker.

Trixie: Why?

Me: Because I asked her to.

Trixie: Whatever. It was because of
Mouton.

Me (*thinking of a comeback and
failing*): Whatever.

Trixie: Don't act like you're not
scared of him.

Me: Why would I be scared of him?

Trixie: Because he's, like, five times
bigger than you.

Me (*closing my locker gently because
my mom takes care of the school*):
I'm not scared of anything.

So even Trixie Longburger knows I'm scared of
Mouton. Is that such a bad thing, though? The entire
seventh grade is afraid of him.

I mean, isn't it cool to do what everyone else is
doing? I guess not, when it involves bravery, courage,
and standing up for yourself.

Soar

Conversation with Trixie—Part II

Trixie: See Mouton lately?

Me: (*silence*)

Trixie: Chicken.

Me: You wouldn't go near him either.

Trixie: Yes, I would.

Me: Prove it.

Trixie: Okay. Watch me.

Me: When?

Trixie: Right now.

Me: I'll believe it when I see it.

Trixie: See it, you feathered psycho.

Trixie beelines to Mouton's locker.

Mouton is there, flinging books from his locker, looking for something. "Has anyone seen my lunch?" he shouts.

Trixie taps him on the shoulder.

Mouton turns from his locker. He towers over her. "You should close your mouth while chewing gum. No, wait. You should close your mouth ALL the time."

For once Mouton has said what everyone else is thinking.

Trixie bites her bottom lip. She looks like she's

about to explode into tears. She picks Mouton's science textbook up off the tile floor. Then she lifts the thick book over her head and belts him across the shoulder with it.

Mouton loses his balance and falls sideways. His head smacks off the lockers, and he drops to the floor. He stays there and doesn't move.

Trixie lets the science book fall from her hand. She huffs and starts to say something, but then hurries off while looking innocent.

If it weren't for his stomach moving up and down when he breathes, I'd bet Mouton was dead.

Mrs. Hughes walks up in her high heels. Her hair is tied up in a bun. It looks like a Buck Burger sitting on her head. Her glasses make her look serious and stern, but everyone knows she's a pushover.

Last year Mouton flushed a stink bomb down the toilet and flooded the sixth-grade hallway. He cried in Mrs. Hughes's office, saying he'd done it to gain more friends. She let him off the hook. No detention. No suspension. Not even a call home to his mom.

"Eddie, what happened?" Mrs. Hughes says. "Is Mouton okay?"

I shrug. "I don't know."

Soar

Mrs. Hughes shakes Mouton. "Mouton? Mouton? Can you hear me?"

Mouton sits up. He's kind of wobbly, and his eyes wander around the hallway. "Science book! Yip-yip!"

"Mouton!" Mrs. Hughes says. "How many fingers am I holding up?" She holds up three fingers.

"Two," Mouton says. "Maybe three."

A crowd begins to gather around us.

Mrs. Hughes turns to me. "Eddie, will you please help me walk him to the nurse?"

I stand there, frozen. I'd rather chew a piece of gum off the ground than help Mouton.

"Eddie, please help me," Mrs. Hughes says.

I don't have a choice. I feel like I have to help, since my mom works at the school and talks to Mrs. Hughes almost every day.

Mrs. Hughes and I each take an arm and lift Mouton off the floor.

I use my other hand to support Mouton's weight, but when I grab on to his body, my hand accidentally slips into a pool of wet T-shirt, otherwise known as Mouton's armpit.

I quickly yank my hand away. Mouton buckles and falls to the floor, pulling Mrs. Hughes down with him.

Mrs. Hughes shrieks.

Mouton shrieks.

Everyone gasps.

From the floor Mrs. Hughes straightens her glasses. "Eddie, what are you doing?" She shakes her head and says to everyone standing around us, "Is there anyone here who can help?"

I take a step away from Mrs. Hughes and Mouton. My face starts getting hot. Mouton must weight three times as much as Mrs. Hughes. She could've been seriously hurt.

Chase, an eighth-grade basketball player, steps forward. He has broad shoulders and long arms. "I can help," he says.

"Thank goodness," Mrs. Hughes says. "Chase, take Mouton's arm." Then she looks at me. "Eddie, you stand back."

I shrink back further into the crowd, bumping into a red dress.

"Excuse you, Eddie," Gabriela says.

Oh great. Gabriela saw the whole thing. No one wants to be best friends with someone who lets the principal down in front of half the school.

Mouton stumbles down the hallway, most of his weight leaning on Chase.

Soar

Mrs. Hughes holds one of Mouton's arms to make it look like she's doing some of the work, but everyone knows that Chase is the only one strong enough to support Mouton.

I lower my head and slip away from the scene, before I can let anyone else down.

Memories

After the last bell rings, I ride home with Mom. She climbs into the car, her keys clinking together on her hip.

Mom says she has a key to every door in school and that it's one of the perks of being the head janitor. I wish she had a key to unlock other people's minds. Then I'd know what Gabriela thinks of me after seeing me fail in the hallway at school.

Mom shuts the car door, strikes a match, and lights a cigarette. She thinks that matches make cigarettes taste better than lighters do, which is completely weird to me. She cracks her window.

"How was your first day?" She puts the key into the

ignition and turns it. Hoopty's engine grumbles and then starts up.

"Good." I stare out the window, looking for birds.

"Did you see Gabriela? Did you talk to her?"

"Mom, it's only the first day."

"I'm just asking. I want to be sure you're reaching out to people, putting yourself out there. Friends don't just show up on your doorstep, you know."

I roll down the window and breathe in the fresh air. "Well, don't worry. I'm putting myself out there."

She reaches over and runs her hand through my hair. "I just want the best for you. I want you to be happy."

"I know."

I can't help but wonder if this is Mom's way of trying to stay involved in my life. I love her and all, but part of me wishes she'd back off and give me some room to breathe.

Mom inhales from the cigarette and flicks the ashes out the window. "I heard about Mouton."

This catches my attention. I turn toward her, ignoring the mockingbird flying overhead. "What'd you hear?" If Mom already heard about what happened, that means people are making a big deal out of it. Rumors are probably darting through the hallways like falcons dive-bombing for starlings.

"I heard that Mouton fainted in the hallway, and

you tried helping but you dropped him on top of Mrs. Hughes."

"Who told you that?"

"Mrs. Hughes."

"That's not what actually happened." I turn back toward the window, but the mockingbird is long gone.

I can feel Mom looking at me. Out of the corner of my eye I can see the cigarette dangling from her mouth, moving every time she talks. "Then tell me your side of the story. Come on, I want the dirt, the good stuff. You can't let your mom walk those halls without being informed."

"It wasn't that big a deal. Mrs. Hughes asked me to help her, so I did. That's it. There, end of story."

Mom looks at me, then back at the road. "I have another question for you."

We turn into our neighborhood, and I hear the upbeat song of an indigo bunting. It sounds like some- one saying, *Tut? Tut? Hair? Hair? Be it? Be it?* I'm hoping Mom's question has nothing to do with school. It's the first day back, and I'm already sick of that place.

"I'm listening," I say.

"What have you been doing over there at Miss Dorothy's house? You've been spending more time over there than at home."

Soar

The indigo bunting song suddenly stops. "I've been looking for the golden eagle."

Mom takes a long puff from her cigarette and blows it out her window, like she's thinking about whether I should be looking for the golden eagle or not. "I know your father wanted you to see that bird, but I don't think it's coming back, Eddie."

I glare at her, like she was the one who stole my bike. "Dad wouldn't lie about something like this."

Mom puts out her cigarette in the car's ashtray. "You sure about that?"

I understand why Mom is acting this way. She's stressed out. She's been working long hours just to put orange juice in the fridge. I do my best to help around the house, but there's only so much I can do.

"You keep searching, Eddie," she says. "Keep on searching. But if that bird doesn't show up, you know what I'm gonna tell you."

Mom presses the radio button. She turns up a country song about losing everything you own and leaving bad memories behind.

There's one bad memory I wish I could leave behind: Dad flying away forever.

Bird
Talkers

By the end of the week, I work up the courage to go to Gabriela's house and ask her about her first week of school. She's in a new country, a new neighborhood, and has to make all new friends. She could use a shoulder to lean on. Plus, I need to show her that I'm not a total failure, like she saw in the hallway at school.

I walk up to Gabriela's house, and a string of clear whistles—*cheer, cheer, cheer*—comes from a tree.

Before I see the bird, I recognize the call as a northern cardinal.

I look up and find it perching on a branch. It's a

male, bright red, with a pointed crest and black mask. It's cool, for a songbird, and it gives me an idea. The black mask. I might need a disguise like that if I have to get my bike on a rescue mission.

Before I have a chance to ring the doorbell, Gabriela shows up at the screen door. "Eddie?" she asks. "What are you doing here?"

Good question. What AM I doing here?

"I—I wanted to see how your first week went. I've never moved, but it must be tough starting over."

"That is sweet."

At least she still thinks I'm sweet, even after seeing me drop Mouton in the hallway.

"The best part was when you tried to lift Mouton and you let go of him. That was hilarity." She giggles, but then notices that I'm not laughing, so she stops.

"Hilarious," I mutter, looking down.

So much for sweet. She must think I'm a total weakling.

She crosses her arms. "I am glad you are not spying on us today. That is a nice change."

"Ha-ha. Funny," I reply, smiling. "By the way, did you know there's a northern cardinal in your tree?"

"What is a northern cardinal?"

"It's our state bird."

"Does this mean it is protected or something like that?"

"Well, you can't shoot it, if that's what you're wondering. It's a male and it looks cool. I can show it to you."

"Maybe another time. I am helping Papa. He has some friends here."

"Oh, okay." My face becomes warm, and I freeze. This is one of those times when you plan something out in your mind but it doesn't go the way you'd hoped. "I guess I'll see you around, then." I turn to leave.

Gabriela opens the screen door. "Wait. Do you want to stay and meet Papa's friends? I have a feeling that you will like them."

"Um, okay." But I really want to say, "Thought you'd never ask."

Gabriela holds the door open all the way. "Come in."

I step inside the house, and it's eerily quiet. "Where is everyone?"

"This way." Gabriela motions for me to follow her.

She leads me through the living room, toward the covered porch. She opens the back door and we step onto the porch, standing outside a circle of people sitting in chairs. Some are older and gray, others are around Mom's age.

The best part is, each person in the circle has a parrot

perched on his shoulder. Nearly all of the birds are macaws. There's one dark blue hyacinth macaw, three blue-and-gold ones, and two green ones. Then there's Silvio, the only scarlet macaw, who perches on Papa's shoulder.

Gabriela turns to me. "We moved here so Papa could be part of this group. He loves animals, so it makes a perfect fit. Training the birds is like therapy for mute people. It is the only group like this in the western hemisphere."

"The only group in the western hemisphere?"

Gabriela nods, smiling.

"Welcome to our friendship circle," says a lady with a great green macaw standing on her shoulder. "Glad you could join us. Are you also mute?"

She's clearly asking me, so I answer. "No."

"Asking is always the easiest way to find out," she explains. "What's your name?"

"Eddie," I tell her.

"Okay, everyone, let's welcome Eddie to our circle."

She does something in sign language. Her hand motions look like a cross between sewing with a needle and playing air guitar. "All together now, on the count of three. One . . . Two . . ."

On three she says "Welcome, Eddie," and then the birds say something that sounds just like that.

With everyone looking at me, I'm sure my face is the color of Silvio's bright red feathers. "Thanks," I tell everyone. "Glad to be here."

"You're welcome," says the lady. "My name is Carolyn Foster Rosetta Sinclair Mitchell, but you can call me Carol. And we, Mr. Eddie, are the Bird Talkers. Everyone here, except you, me, and Princess Gabriela, is deaf mute. That means they can't hear or talk. Well, let me clarify. Some can hear specific sounds, but none can talk. Would you like to hear the birds talk some more?"

"Sure." I glance at Gabriela. She's obviously amused at the spotlight being thrown on me.

Papa strokes his black beard. I wonder if he can hear me, or if he can only read my lips.

Carol sits up straight and counts to three again, showing the numbers on her fingers. When she says "three," the adults gesture with their right hands, making a sign that resembles their first two fingers going down a waterslide together.

The birds all say, "Groovy."

Carol laughs, and the circle laughs silently. "That is my all-time favorite, Mr. Eddie. That's a silly nilly word. It doesn't get much use in the real world, but it sure provides some laughs for us. Wouldn't you agree?"

I look at Gabriela. We hide our smiles so we don't offend Carol. It's all I can do to not laugh at this whole situation, not in a mean way but in an awesome, I-can't-believe-this-is-happening-to-me way.

After a couple more demonstrations from Carol and the gang, Papa brings out snacks and drinks from the kitchen. I eat a handful of Brazil nuts, then wash them down with one of Papa's delicious berry drinks.

I toss my plastic cup into the recycling container. "I better get home for dinner."

The macaws are amazing, and the truth is, I'd rather stay here than go home, but it's only fair that I show up for dinner. Mom's probably lonely and needs someone to break up the quietness.

Gabriela walks me to the front door.

"That was awesome," I tell her. "You're lucky to have those macaws at your house."

"It is good therapy for them. They have a real connection with the birds. Though Carol can be a lot to handle."

We laugh together.

And that makes me feel like flying.

When I get home, I open my journal and flip to my drawing of Silvio.

It's crazy what you discover about art when you haven't seen it for a while. It's by far the best sketch I've ever done! The head and beak are proportionate, and the feathers are just as colorful and vibrant as Silvio's in real life.

I want to look at the older sketches in my journal, but then I'll be up all night fixing wings and crests and beak shapes. I can't be tired at school, especially during science class.

I turn the page and begin sketching the northern cardinal from Gabriela's front yard. I've seen a lot of them this year, but this one was more impressive than the rest, maybe because it was near Gabriela's house. Everything that comes close to Gabriela seems bigger and better.

Bird: Northern cardinal

Location: Gabriela's front yard (in giant oak tree)

Note: Most impressive northern cardinal seen this year.

Dad: You would flip out over the Bird Talkers.

I've never seen so many colorful feathers in one place.

It makes me wonder about myself.

Am I a colorful person?

Bow Tie—Wearing
Quail Killer

The next Friday, before school starts, I wake up early and head to Miss Dorothy's to look for the golden eagle. I walk around the side of her house, the brown grass crunching under my shoes.

Miss Dorothy leans on a cane behind her screen door. Her white hair matches the house's chipped paint. She waves at me, and I wave back.

"Morning, Miss Dorothy!" I shout.

"Shouldn't you be in school?" she asks.

I look at my watch. "Not for another twenty minutes!"

"Go ahead, Eddie. It's all yours." She smiles and gestures to her backyard, like she has just unveiled a magical forest for the first time.

"Thanks, Miss Dorothy!"

She cups a hand behind one ear. "What did you say?"

I put both hands around my mouth to funnel the sound. "Thanks!"

She turns and hobbles back into the kitchen.

Miss Dorothy can't hear like she used to. It's too bad she's going downhill, because her land is going with her. It used to be nice back here, so nice that Dad would let me swim in the pond. But now the water is low from lack of rain. Besides that, people with nothing better to do sneak back here and throw parties and leave their trash everywhere.

Today an old tennis shoe and a Doritos bag float on the water. Plastic bags and soggy cardboard boxes sit at the pond's edge. And then there's that dead fish smell, which never goes away.

Still, there are enough rabbits, mice, and other small rodents here to keep raptors happy, and that's what matters to me.

I circle the pond and head toward the railroad tracks. The tracks mark the end of Miss Dorothy's land.

Soar

Coop likes to perch on the telephone poles back there, so I might catch her chasing down breakfast.

When I get to the tracks, there's no sign of Coop anywhere. Maybe she's still sleeping, or maybe she's already tracked down a sparrow.

I search the ground for traces of the golden eagle. All I find is a rusted coffee can and an old bicycle. I kick the can, and it tumbles forward, clanking off a hollow log. The bicycle hides down in the brush. It's been out here so long that it's hard to tell the paint from the rust.

BANG!

I hit the ground and cover my head!

BANG!

Gunshots?

Someone is shooting!

I look around and then bolt for cover under an elm tree. I stay low and wait, breathing hard, trying to control my thumping heart.

No more shots are fired, so I run around the pond to where I think the shots came from. The pond's far side is empty, so I scamper past more trees, all the way to the railroad tracks. Squatting behind a log, I brace for another gunshot.

But there's only silence.

I wonder where Coop is, and if she's okay.

I hide in the brush, my head sticking out far enough to follow the tracks. A man stands on the railroad tracks, about three robins' nests away. He wears a camouflage jacket and pants, and a bright orange hat. He points the shotgun into the air.

BANG!

A northern bobwhite stops midflight, free-falls from the sky, and lands between two railroad ties.

It's the first time I've ever seen a person shoot a living thing, and it's a bird. I swallow twice to keep my throat from getting dry.

The hunter leans the shotgun against his leg and turns up his jacket collar.

I move back into the brush, out of sight, until I can figure out who's hunting on Miss Dorothy's land.

The hunter walks my way, holding the shotgun across his chest like a soldier. As he gets closer, I notice he's wearing a camouflage bow tie.

It's Mr. Dover!

But that doesn't make sense. Mr. Dover loves birds. He's helping Zeus recover from his broken wing. How can he be out here killing quail?

I can't let Mr. Dover strut past me without saying

something to him, especially after that whole speech about the lightning storm and saving Zeus's life. What would Zeus think of all this? His own savior out killing his distant cousins?

I stay low, hidden in the brush. The tall, bristly grass reminds me of a jail cell, and that's about how I feel right now. Like a prisoner, trapped in Mr. Dover's bird-killing dream.

Mr. Dover stops walking and drops to one knee. A golden retriever bounds down the tracks, tongue hanging out, like Gabriela's dog when it yanked me off her fence.

The dog leaps into Mr. Dover's lap. He pets the dog's head and says "good boy" over and over until I think he's never going to say anything else.

Then he says, "Apollo, go get it," and the dog bounds toward the quail, snatches it up, and brings it back to Mr. Dover.

My bottom jaw hangs loose. Since when is it okay for your science teacher to shoot a bird and then order his dog to retrieve the carcass for him?

Mr. Dover stands up and walks toward where I'm hiding.

I wipe my sweaty hands on my shorts. Then I take a deep breath and whisper to myself, "You can do this."

Apollo runs his nose over the tracks. He scampers a few more feet and sniffs the grass. He comes closer, possibly tracking my scent.

Before I can talk myself out of it, I stand up.

"What are you doing here?" I ask him.

Mr. Dover looks at me, surprised, holding the limp quail by the neck. "Eddie?"

"Why are you killing birds?"

He puts one hand in the air. "Eddie, wait. It's not what it seems."

"Really? Because it seems like you're out here wasting quail and making your dog round them up for you. *And* you're on Miss Dorothy's land. I thought you had your own *property*." I clench my teeth.

"Eddie, please, let me explain."

Apollo trots over to me and weaves in and out of my legs, but he's more curious than aggressive.

"My dad was right. You're a fake." I storm away, hoping to never see Mr. Dover or a dead bird again.

Mr. Dover calls after me. "You're the fake, Eddie."

Chicken Patty
Tuesday

I stop in my tracks. Apollo weaves around my legs again, then runs off to chase something in the tall grass.

I turn around, facing Mr. Dover. "Me? I don't go around talking about birds like they're the greatest creatures on earth and then use them for target practice."

"Quail hunting is a sport, Eddie. I eat what I kill."

The word "kill" rings in my head. He's a murderer, and he's admitting it. How can this quail killer be my science teacher?

"A sport? What kind of sport ends in death?"

"Do you eat lunch at school, Eddie?"

"Changing the subject isn't going to convince me."
I know what Mr. Dover is trying to do, and he's not going
to persuade me to see his side of the story.

"No, really. Stay with me, Eddie. Do you eat lunch at
school or bring it from home? Just answer the question."

"I eat at school," I tell him.

"What about Tuesdays? Do you eat cafeteria food
on Tuesdays?"

"I eat lunch there every day."

"Then you're a murderer too. And you don't even
realize it."

"I don't get it. What are you talking about?"

"Chicken patties. Every Tuesday you eat a chicken
patty for lunch. Delivered to the school in boxes from
freezer trucks. You know where those chicken patties
come from?"

I think about that for a second. "No."

"The Brownsville Slaughter Grounds."

Apollo circles Mr. Dover's feet and licks the toe of
his boot.

"Eddie, those chicken patties start as real, live
chickens. Do you know how they kill chickens at the
Brownsville Slaughter Grounds?"

I stand there, listening, but don't say anything. Mr.

Dover must be smart enough to figure out that this means I don't know the answer.

"There are these kids who work there. They're about your age or maybe even a little younger. They run around the pen chasing down chickens and grabbing them by their hind legs. When they catch one, they bring it over to a tree stump, where a man in a white suit—usually his name is something like Jeb—kindly thanks the kid for bringing him the chicken. Sometimes Jeb even gives the kid a piece of candy for doing his job properly."

I shrug. "Lucky kid."

"Then Jeb slams the chicken onto a tree stump and pins it down by the neck. The chicken squirms and squawks and pleads for help. But Jeb has a job to do. He raises an axe and chops the chicken's head off. He pitches the head into a bucket and then frees the body. The chicken runs around headless for a few minutes while the kids laugh and point at it. It knocks other chickens over, like it's all a big game of blind chicken bumper cars. Then it falls over and bleeds to death. And that, Eddie, that headless body, is what you eat between two buns on Tuesdays."

Axes? Jeb? Headless chickens? Kids laughing? Mr.

Dover tells the story so casually that it makes my stomach turn. It's like he's been there to see it all happen.

After hearing the story about Jeb, I can barely get words out. "Whatever. Frozen chicken patties are different."

"Jeb kills chicken, you eat chicken. I shoot quail, I eat quail. There's no difference, Eddie." He adjusts the shotgun, holding it across his chest the other way.

Apollo must sense that Mr. Dover's story is over. He darts toward an opening in the brush. He leaps over the tracks and disappears behind a wall of overgrown grass that's as tall as me.

"Eddie, I've been honest about why I'm here. But what exactly are *you* doing here?"

I tell him the truth. "I'm looking for the golden eagle."

Mr. Dover smirks. "Oh, Eddie. You have a higher probability of finding a grizzly out here than a golden eagle."

My heart speeds up. "How do you know?"

"Every scientist knows that strong data leads to an accurate hypothesis. There's never been an official golden eagle sighting in this town."

"Yes, there has. My dad saw one right here. It had

wings wider than a creek and talons the size of bulldozer claws. And it had a gray spot on its wing. I swear, he saw it right here."

"Eddie. I know plenty of birders in this town, some of them professionals. Do you really believe a golden eagle that big could fly through this town without anyone else seeing it?"

"My dad wasn't a liar." My heart won't slow down. It feels like it's sprouting wings and about to burst out of my chest.

Apollo comes bouncing from the tall grass.

Miss Dorothy hobbles out behind the dog, steadying herself with her cane. She looks mad at the world.

Dire Consequence

Miss Dorothy is wearing a bright pink robe, and she's barefoot! How did she make it barefoot from her house all the way to the railroad tracks?

Apollo runs up to her, his tail wagging back and forth, slapping Miss Dorothy's legs.

"Shoo!" She motions for Apollo to get lost. "Get outta here, Old Yeller."

Apollo turns and runs over to Mr. Dover, his tongue hanging out, his yellow fur shining in the morning sun.

Mr. Dover takes one of Miss Dorothy's arms to help her.

"Shoo!" she says again. "I don't need your help.

Who are you anyway? And what's with all the boom noise out here?"

Mr. Dover walks alongside her. "I'm Lamb Dover. I was clearing out quail for you. They wreak havoc if you let them overpopulate."

"Lamb?" Miss Dorothy questions. "Your mother must've hated you. I bet you came out screaming and peeing all over the place. As quiet as a lamb." She laughs at her own joke. I kind of laugh too.

Mr. Dover holds the quail by its short neck, showing it to Miss Dorothy. "See this bird? If quail overpopulate, they can suffer dire consequences. Lack of primary resources, limited nesting habitats, these factors can cause territorial distress and lead to—"

"Oh, please," Miss Dorothy interrupts. "I've lived in this house since I was twelve. I grew up with these quail. You're the only dire consequence I've seen come through here in eighty years."

Mr. Dover reaches down and rubs Apollo's head. "Quail populations depend on us, don't they, boy?"

"Listen here, Lamb Man." Miss Dorothy steadies herself with her cane while pointing a finger at Mr. Dover. "I don't care what you're shooting. I don't want to see you on my land again. And for heaven's sake, take that hideous bow tie off. There are some things my little Eddie shouldn't see."

I can tell by the way Mr. Dover sticks out his chin that he wants to defend himself. Instead he looks at me. "See you in class, Eddie." He starts down the tracks. "Come on, boy," he says, and Apollo trots after him.

Once Mr. Dover is out of sight, I walk with Miss Dorothy toward her house, giving her my arm to lean on.

"Oh, Eddie, I used to love seeing you here with your dad," she says. "He was such a good man."

"Miss Dorothy?" I pause, deciding how to ask what I'm about to ask.

"What is it, Eddie?"

"Was my dad . . ." I swallow hard, unable to finish my thought.

"Go on, spit it out," she says.

"Was he an honest person?" I finally ask her.

She stops walking.

A northern bobwhite runs across the ground in front of us. With three quick wing beats, the quail flies away, taking cover in the trees.

"Put it this way," she says. "Your father was his own person. He was true to himself. The way I see it, that's as honest as one can be."

I nod. "Thanks, Miss Dorothy."

She takes hold of my arm, and we walk the rest of the way to her house.

As I'm walking toward the bus stop, the bus belches smoke from its tailpipe and leaves me behind in a dark cloud. I could chase the bus down, but what's the point? I'd rather get pegged with dodge balls in PE than sit in Mr. Dover's science class.

From the back of the bus, Mouton sticks his head out the window. "Eddie-shovel-truck! Eddie-shovel-truck! Yip-yip!"

I want to yell something back at Mouton—like Dad did once when he told another birder who wouldn't get out of his way to "Move it or lose 'em," in reference to the guy's teeth—but then Mouton will mess with my locker or do something worse.

It's smarter to ignore him, so that's what I do.

After catching Mr. Dover in the act of killing quail, I have a bad feeling about school. Will Mr. Dover call on me in front of everyone? Will he make my tests harder on purpose? Will he tell my mom about what happened this morning at Miss Dorothy's place?

I walk to school, thinking about that quail falling

from the sky. Then I imagine the same thing happening
to my science grade.

Bird: Northern bobwhite
Location: Miss Dorothy's place
Note: Mr. Dover is a hypocrite. Do not trust him.
Dad: Miss Dorothy says you were true to your-
   self. I believe her.
But is that the same as being an honest person?

Symposium Nightmare

A week goes by, and the whole time I stay low-key in science class. I don't look at Mr. Dover, and he doesn't look at me.

Mr. Dover straightens his canary-yellow bow tie. "Today you will be assigned your partner for the symposium project."

His mouth keeps moving, but I don't hear anything after the word "project."

Killer.

Murderer.

Liar.

Those are the only words that come to mind.

Mr. Dover continues. "And did you know, ladies and gentlemen of the seventh grade, that we are in the presence of greatness. Well, actually the heir of greatness. Eddie here is the son of a birding legend."

My face gets hot and my neck itches. Why is he dragging *me* into this? If anyone deserves a hot face and an itchy neck, it's *him*, not me.

"Eddie, why don't you tell the class about your father's symposium project? After all, he was famous around West Plains."

I know exactly what this is about.

"That's okay," I respond. "Maybe another time."

From the front row Gabriela turns around and looks at me. "I would like to hear about your father's project."

First Mr. Dover, now Gabriela? What's going on here?

"No, really," I insist. "I don't feel like talking about it."

"Please, Eddie." Gabriela smiles.

I have to admit, Gabriela's smile is hard to resist. And if I want to have friends, then I have to put myself out there, like Mom said.

"Okay," I agree.

I tell the story about Dad's project, how he took home a blue ribbon the size of a grandfather clock, which still hangs in Mom's bedroom.

Soar

Dad's project was so good that it gained attention from regional birding groups, it earned him a full-length feature in *BirdWatching* magazine, and a reporter from *National Geographic* came to school and wrote an article about him.

Dad was even interviewed on the local news channel!

He also won a two-hundred-and-fifty-dollar scholarship that he never used, because he didn't go to college. He said college was for smart people, and that he wasn't smart but full of enough common sense to feed logic to seven smart people for a lifetime. I'm not sure I understood what he meant by saying all that, but it sounded good.

Dad's project poster board now sits in the garage, tucked away in a corner, collecting dust and spiderwebs.

When I finish telling the class about Dad's project, Gabriela smiles, like she's satisfied or maybe even impressed. Now if only I could rig today's drawing so we could be symposium project partners. That could be the first step in a friendship that could last forever.

"Inspiring story, Eddie," Mr. Dover says. I can't tell if he's being serious or sarcastic. "I can't wait to see how much of your father's talent rubbed off on you."

He takes a robin's nest off the counter. "Now for the partner drawing. Remember, it doesn't matter who your partner is, or if you have a past with this person, positive or negative. We start over in seventh grade. The slate is wiped clean. It's important to respect your partner's opinions and abilities in order to produce the best project."

How can Mr. Dover talk about respect? What about respect for birds?

"The first symposium pairing is . . ." He reaches into the robin's nest and pulls out two folded slips of paper. "Trixie . . ."

Trixie grins, showing off her orange braces.

Mr. Dover unfolds the second piece of paper. "And Gabriela."

My pencil breaks on a page in my bird journal. For the first time ever, I wish I had orange hair and braces, and my name was Trixie Longburger.

Mr. Dover pulls a few more pairings from the robin's nest. I don't pay attention. I'm too busy drawing a picture inspired by the Grim Quail-Reaper.

I sketch a giant quail the size of a *T. rex*. It has one foot raised high in the air, and it's about to stomp on Mr. Dover's house. I draw Mr. Dover's house as a one-story ranch style on a big property, just as I remember driving past it with Dad.

There's one detail in the picture I'm really proud of. I've drawn Zeus, the American kestrel, in the top corner of the page. I make it obvious that he gets away safely, out of Quailzilla's path of destruction.

"Eddie."

I look up.

Mr. Dover is staring at me while holding a tiny slip of paper. He has drawn my name from the robin's nest. I close my bird journal so no one can see the Quailzilla picture.

Mr. Dover mixes up the papers in the nest. "Let's see who will be the lucky partner with the heir of greatness."

He pulls out the crinkled slip of paper, unfolds it, and says one name.

"Mouton."

Woodpecker Pens and Bird Wars

The first thing that goes through my mind is that Mr. Dover has paired me with Mouton on purpose. This can't be accidental. Stepping on a toddler's foot while standing in line at the wild bird exhibit is an accident. But being partnered with Mouton for a science project, after my run-in with Mr. Dover, is definitely not an accident.

I can't believe this. I'll have to pull off a miracle to win the blue ribbon.

Mr. Dover drops the paper strip on the counter. He draws more names but I'm not listening.

"Okay, everyone. Partner up. Make a list of five

possibilities for your symposium project. Remember, you're going to be working closely with this person, so make sure you both agree on your choices. Stubbornness and arguing will only make your lives miserable."

Yeah, he definitely partnered me with Mouton on purpose. "Miserable" is going to be my middle name.

Mouton taps his woodpecker pen on his desk. "Eddie-shovel-truck! Eddie-shovel-truck!"

Mouton got this woodpecker pen in fourth grade, the same year he started calling me Fish Boy. The pen is red and black. In the top part is a small red-headed woodpecker figurine that floats in clear liquid. He showed up to class with the pen one day, and he kept tapping it on his notebook. The tapping was just loud enough to be annoying, but Mrs. Rollins didn't take the pen away from him. Maybe she thought it would give him something to focus on, other than blurting out "Yip!" in the middle of spelling lessons.

Everyone in class stands up and moves next to their partners.

Gabriela sits next to Trixie, who's chewing gum and talking so fast, you can't understand her.

Mouton drums his woodpecker pen on his notebook. The drumming gets louder every year. I can tell that he's never going to move closer to me, and I'm not going closer to him, so instead I stare at my bird journal and pretend I didn't hear Mr. Dover's instructions.

"Eddie," Mr. Dover says. "Mouton is waiting for you."

I roll my eyes, without Mr. Dover seeing me.

I should've stayed hidden in the tall brush at Miss Dorothy's place, and then none of this would've ever happened. I'd be partners with Gabriela, not Mouton. Gabriela would listen to my ideas about the science symposium and smile at me. We'd agree on our project and carry out our plan like two scientists. Like two friends.

I pull out a chair and plop down next to Mouton.

"Eddie-shovel-truck!" He taps the pen on his notebook, the woodpecker dancing up and down in the clear liquid part.

"I can't believe we're partners," I say.

Mouton leans over close to me. "So, Bird Nerd. Are your legs tired from walking everywhere?"

I glare at him. "So you *do* have my bike."

"I didn't say that. Yip!"

"I'm coming to get it back, Mouton, if it's the last thing I ever do on earth."

"Try it. I dare you."

Before I explode in anger, I pull out a piece of paper and scribble "Symposium" at the top. "I have an idea for our project. I've had this idea for a long time, and you're not going to mess it up."

My pencil lead breaks on the paper. I get up to sharpen it. "I'll be right back."

I walk past Gabriela. She holds out her arm and stops me. "Sorry about your partner."

I shrug. "It's okay."

But it's not okay. I want to say this stinks like a skunk, but I figure that doesn't fall under "putting myself out there."

When I get back to my seat, Mouton is rolling the pen back and forth on the desk. "I have an idea," he says.

"Great. I can't wait to hear it."

"We can make a poster of woodpecker pens. We'll order one from every state." He holds up the pen. The woodpecker floats up and down, then side to side.

"Are you kidding me? We're not doing that. And not every state sells those pens."

"How do you know?"

"I just know!"

I write down my symposium idea and slide the paper over to him.

He reads it over. "You write sloppy."

I snatch the paper away from him. "We're going to hypothesize that a golden eagle lives right here in West Plains, and then we're going to prove it. That's our project."

Mouton folds his arms over his chest. "Woodpecker-woodpecker-woodpecker."

At the end of class Mr. Dover collects the papers. When he gets to me, he stops. "How did your first brainstorm session go?"

"Great." I hold out the paper. At the top is my paragraph explaining the golden eagle project. "This is our official proposal."

Mr. Dover skims my paper, then looks at me. "I'll have to approve this topic before you can take it any further. As for Mouton's idea, I'll need a hieroglyphics expert to read it."

"It says woodpecker pens," I explain. "It's not that hard to read."

Sticking up for Mouton seems like the only thing to do. I can't let Mr. Dover think he's getting the best of me by pairing me with Mouton on purpose.

The bird clock chirps.

Soar

Mr. Dover turns to the class. "Time's up, everyone. See you tomorrow."

I go back to my seat and open my bird journal. I rip out the drawing of Quailzilla's destruction and fold it in half.

On my way out of class, when no one's looking, I drop the folded drawing onto Mr. Dover's desk. Mr. Dover probably thinks he can keep me from winning the blue ribbon at the science symposium.

This makes me think about Dad and what he would do in this situation. I think the first thing he would do is remind me of rule number three: No one gets in your way.

Let the bird wars begin.

Order and Progress

On Saturday morning, I walk up the driveway to Gabriela's house. Papa is trimming bushes with hedge clippers. He stops, holding the clippers in one hand, and waves. Silvio perches on his shoulder, staring at me. I knock on the door and wait. From the yard Silvio gives me the stink eye.

Finally Gabriela comes to the door. "Eddie? What are you doing here again?"

Again? What's that supposed to mean? Is she keeping track of how many times I show up at her house?

"Sorry to stop by like this, but I need help." I try looking desperate.

"Help with what? You need to be exactly."

"You mean 'exact.'"

"Right." Gabriela rolls her eyes.

I could kick myself for correcting her English. Who wants a friend correcting you all the time? "I need help with my symposium project."

"You? The Heir of Greatness? I am surprised. I did not think you would even need a partner."

"Well, Mouton's not exactly a partner."

"He is better than nothing. Right?"

"If only I could find something Mouton is good at besides saying 'Eddie-shovel-truck' all the time. So will you help me out?"

Gabriela opens the screen door and signs something to Papa. He nods and signs back to her. "I would be happy to help you, Eddie. Come in."

As we walk through the house toward the back porch, a familiar smell hits me. A huge pot sits on the stove. Papa must be cooking up another batch of his special berry drink.

On the back porch the circle of chairs is still set up from Carol and the Bird Talkers. Also, four ruby-throated hummingbirds dart around the honeysuckle bush, near the privacy fence. Last time I was back here, I didn't notice the bush *or* the hummingbirds. I guess the Bird Talkers distracted me.

Gabriela begins stacking the chairs. "The *beija-flores* are cute."

"The what?"

"I mean, the *birds*."

"Yeah, they're ruby-throated hummingbirds. They're common around here. I'm surprised you have so many. They're usually territorial."

"They must like us." Smiling, she stacks two more chairs.

I pick up two chairs and swing them over my head. I stumble, then regain my balance. I stack the chairs on top of the others.

"Thank you for helping me. Now, will you tell me about your symposium project?" She smiles.

"Sure. That's why I'm here. It always helps to talk about plans with someone else."

We stack the last few chairs, go inside, and sit on the couch.

Gabriela turns to me. "Okay, I am ready. I want to hear all about it."

I take a deep breath. "Well, my hypothesis states that a golden eagle exists right here in West Plains.

So basically, the purpose of my project is to find that bird."

"How do you plan to find it?"

"First I'll need a spool of string and six tree branches to set squirrel traps. I'll use the dead squirrel to attract the golden eagle, because eagles are known to scavenge while migrating."

"Scavenge?"

"It means they eat anything they can find, even if it's already dead."

Gabriela takes out her notebook. She writes the word "scavenge" and the definition.

"I'll also need my bike to get around town faster, my binoculars, a mini flashlight, and my mom's cross pouch to carry materials and evidence."

"What is a cross pouch?"

"It's a bag you wear around your waist. It's actually called a fanny pack, but I don't call it that. It sounds too wimpy."

Gabriela leans forward, resting her chin in her hand. "Out of all the birds, why did you choose the golden eagle?"

"Because I've been looking for it since before my dad flew away."

"Flew away?"

"My dad is gone. It happened last year."

She sets her notebook on the couch and puts the cap on her pen. She glances down. "I am sorry, Eddie. I did not know this."

We both sit there in the living room, in the same place where she held an ice pack on my injured head, where I saw her big brown eyes up close for the first time. On that day there was comfort and a welcoming face hovering above me. Now there's nothing but silence.

My bottom lip trembles. Sometimes my emotions come out when I don't expect them to, especially when I talk about Dad. This is one of those times.

Gabriela notices. "It is okay. You have feelings inside you, and you need to let them free. Papa tells me it is okay to act this way after you lose something important."

The way Gabriela talks, Papa must know a lot about life. I wish Mom would say things like that. Maybe then she'd talk more about Dad, instead of hardly mentioning him.

I reel my emotions in, and my bottom lip goes back to normal. "When did your father tell you that?"

Gabriela looks down, then at me. "I have lost something too, Eddie." She fiddles with the orange pen in her hand. "I lost my mother when I was three. She became very sick with an infection, and we did not have good medicines where I am from in Brazil. We lived far away from the city. The doctors could do nothing for her."

"Wow," I say quietly. "I'm sorry."

"Eddie." She sets the pen on the table. "I will help you with your project. I believe you can find this golden eagle."

"Thanks. But technically you're not allowed to help me. I'm supposed to do the project with Mouton, or the judges can disqualify us. It's in the rules."

"Then why did you come to my door?"

"I don't know. Maybe I just wanted to talk. Or maybe I need some luck."

Gabriela smiles. "Do you think I am lucky?"

I say the only thing that comes to mind. "Anyone who attracts that many hummingbirds *must* be lucky."

Gabriela looks down. I've made her blush, but it seems like a good blush, like my face after someone says my bird drawing is awesome, or my faded Black Crowes T-shirt is cool, which doesn't happen very often.

"You are definitely sweet," she says.

I look up at Gabriela. Behind her, on the wall, hangs the green-and-yellow Brazilian flag. I wonder about the words on the white band streaming across the blue circle.

"What do those words mean?" I point at the flag.

"*Ordem e Progresso.* 'Order and progress.' Those are words we live by in Brazil. It comes from positivism. Love, order, and progress. We had to memorize it in my school."

"What's positivism?"

"I do not remember much about this. One part says that real truth is *only* found in science. But I do not believe that is true." She looks at the flag, then at me. "Do you think that is true?"

I think about those words for a long moment.

Truth. Science. Believe.

I lean back against the couch and hold a pillow on my lap, protecting me like a shield. "I don't know."

Operation Ninja Bird

So what is the first step for your project?" Gabriela asks me.

"I need to get my bike back from Mouton. That way I can cruise around town and gather things I need. My mom works late. She doesn't have time to take me all over the place. Plus I can't keep it from my mom much longer. She's going to figure it out sooner or later."

Gabriela stands up, smoothing out her dress. "Would you like a cup of Papa's berry drink?"

"Right now?"

"Eddie, we have a plan to make. You could be here for a while. We need strength."

Be here for a while? There's no place I'd rather be right now than Gabriela's living room, sipping Papa's berry drink.

"Sure, I'll have some. Maybe it'll help us think better."

Gabriela brings two drinks from the kitchen and sets them on the table. Steam rises from the cups. The smell is stronger than I remember. "This one is made from the camu camu berry. It is high in vitamin C. Papa says it gives you strength and courage."

"Courage," I say, rubbing my hands together. "Sounds like a winner to me."

She drops the orange pen and her notebook into my lap. "You will be the note-taker."

"Um, okay." I open the notebook's flowery cover and uncap the pen. "What does that make you?"

Gabriela sips her camu camu drink like a cup of hot soup. "I am the rhyme and the reason."

"Rhyme and reason? Where did you hear that?"

"From this book." She holds up a torn-up, crinkled paperback. *The Phantom Tollbooth*. The corners are creased, and a few pages are dog-eared.

"I read that in fifth grade."

"I know. This is *your* book. Your mother brought over a box of gifts the day after we moved in. This book was in the box. You have so many strange phrases in English. It is hard to keep track of them. I am trying to learn them all."

"So, wait, you're learning better English by reading *The Phantom Tollbooth*?"

"Yes."

"Okay, whatever you say."

"Is this another phrase I should know? 'Whatever you say'?"

"Actually, yes. It means 'whatever you just said is good enough for me.'" I tap the pen on Gabriela's notebook, which reminds me of Mouton and his nervous tapping in class. Now that I think about it, the tapping is easy to do, especially when your mind is on more important matters, like telling your new friend what overused phrases mean.

In the notebook I write "Golden Plan" at the top of the first page.

Together we come up with a list of plans to get my bike back.

1. **Operation Nuns Saving Orphaned Babies.**
    Gabriela dresses up like a nun. She distracts
    Mouton at the front door while I sneak around

back, hop the fence, snatch my Predator (assuming it's somewhere in the backyard), lift it over the fence, and then hop back over to safety and ride my bike into the night, all while Gabriela wraps up her speech on saving orphaned babies.

Positives: Low cost, just a nun costume.

Negatives: There's a chance my bike will not be in the backyard, and this plan does not give me time to look anywhere else.

2. **Operation Woodpecker Pens.** I order woodpecker pens from different states (if they exist) and tape them to a poster board. I knock on Mouton's door, then run and hide. Gabriela will be stationed at her place on the street. When Mouton answers the door, Gabriela walks by holding the poster so Mouton can see all the woodpecker pens. Mouton will come after Gabriela and he'll want to see the pens up close. Gabriela's job is to keep walking, away from the house. Mouton will be so distracted by the pens that he'll tag along. Once they're far enough away from the house, I make my move. I run inside

the house, avoiding Mouton's parents (might be better to wait until Mouton is home alone), find my Predator, and ride off in the opposite direction, away from Mouton and Gabriela.

Positives: The house becomes an empty nest, so I have more time to look for my Predator.

Negatives: Mouton annoys Gabriela. She has to listen to him go on and on about woodpecker pens.

3. **Operation Ninja Bird.** Gabriela acts as the lookout. She dresses in black and stations herself behind the big oak tree in Mouton's front yard. We communicate through the Donald Duck walkie-talkies that Timmy Latham's little brother left behind. I wear my fifth-grade Halloween ninja costume. Actually, I call it the Ninja Bird costume, because I was a ninja with an eagle for a sidekick. I sneak into Mouton's backyard and look for my bike. If I do not locate my bike in the backyard, I'll be forced to search deeper, possibly looking into Mouton's windows. Once I locate my bike,

I will take it and sneak away, without being noticed.

Positives: Gabriela does not have to inter-act with Mouton. She stays safe, behind the oak tree.

Negatives: None. Ninjas are never heard or seen.

Epic Quailzilla
Destruction

During the first week of October, Mr. Dover weaves through the aisles, passing back symposium project proposals. His bow tie is a swirly mess of colors: red, blue, and yellow. He calls it his Brazilian bow tie because he thinks the colors represent a scarlet macaw.

Gabriela says the colors aren't the same. According to her, the blue is too light, the yellow too bright, and the red is not red at all. It's burgundy.

Mr. Dover finishes passing back all the papers. "I've approved most of your proposals with an owl stamp that says 'Hoot, hoot.' Otherwise, Mr. Squirrel stamp is telling you to 'Get crackin',' which means back to the drawing board in squirrel talk."

But there's a problem. Mouton and I didn't get our proposal back. Mr. Dover must have forgotten to pass out our paper. Maybe it's so good that he wants to frame it and hang it behind his desk.

Doubt it.

I raise my hand.

Mr. Dover ignores me. He uncaps the green marker and writes "Teamwork" on the white board. "This isn't basketball, where you have to work the ball around the perimeter to find the player who's open or the player who can take advantage of a mismatch. And it's not a theater production, where the lights operator is just as important as the lead actor, because without lights there's no acting to be seen, and without acting there's no production."

I keep my hand in the air. I'm not giving up. I want to know about my proposal.

"This is a science project. One that's conceived, planned, and executed by you *and* your partner."

I support my arm that's in the air with my other arm. The blood drains from my fingertips to my shoulder.

Finally he calls on me. "Eddie."

"I just want to know where our—"

"Eddie, I'll speak to you after class." He cuts me off before I can finish.

Mouton drums the woodpecker pen on his desk. "Eddie-shovel-truck!"

From across the room Gabriela finds me and opens her eyes wide. She must know I'm in trouble.

I spend the rest of class tuning out and secretly drawing a peregrine falcon in my bird journal. The peregrine falcon is one of the most underrated birds. It's a small raptor and can dive-bomb from its perch at two hundred miles per hour. I wish they lived in Indiana. It's no golden eagle, but any bird that looks like it has a mustache must be cool.

The bird clock chirps.

Mr. Dover says "Time's up" and dismisses everyone.

On her way out Gabriela walks past me and leans into my ear. "Do not bite off more than you can chew."

The classroom finally empties.

Mr. Dover walks toward me, and I close my bird journal. He lets a piece of paper fall from his hand, and it lands crookedly on my desk.

It's my drawing of Quailzilla.

I stare at my drawing.

"Tell me, Eddie, who would draw something like this?"

"I don't know. Mouton?"

He smirks, and I can feel he's getting frustrated with me. "I thought we were going to make this a good year?"

"That was the plan, until you made Mouton my partner."

"The partner drawings were completely random, Eddie. You saw the robin's nest."

"I wish I could believe you." I start loading my books into my backpack. "You know something, Mr. Dover, I don't think you really *knew* my dad."

"I knew him well enough to know that you're following in his footsteps."

"What's that supposed to mean?"

"Eddie, your dad said he saw a golden eagle in October. That's not possible. They only come around these parts in the winter. And even then, it would be unheard of to see a bird like that."

I shove my bird journal into my backpack, leaving the Quailzilla drawing on my desk. I want to take the drawing with me, but I can't bring myself to admit that it's mine.

Soar

"If you knew my dad so well, then what was his favorite bird?"

"I assume it was the golden eagle."

"Wrong. It was actually the sharp-shinned hawk."

Mr. Dover holds up another piece of paper and lets it fall onto my desk. It glides over the Quailzilla drawing, covering everything except Quailzilla's beak.

It's our project proposal, with an owl stamp at the top.

"Hoot, hoot," Mr. Dover says. "You won't find a golden eagle, but I'm going to let you spread your wings and give it a go."

"So you're approving our project?"

"Absolutely. However, I do expect you to utilize every step of the scientific method. And remember, there are rules for the symposium. Mouton is your partner, and he *must* contribute to the project in a real way. Otherwise you'll be disqualified."

I nod in agreement. "Thanks."

I begin to leave and brush past Mr. Dover.

"Eddie." I turn back, and he's holding out my Quailzilla drawing. "You forgot your bird monster."

There's no use faking it anymore. I take the drawing from him.

"It's not a bird monster. It's Quailzilla."

Operation Ninja
Bird. Over.

The next day during science class I get up to sharpen my pencil. I walk past Gabriela and say, "It's time to put Operation Ninja Bird into action."

"When?" she asks.

"Tonight."

Gabriela nods. "Okay."

"Back to your seat, Eddie." Mr. Dover stands at the front of the classroom.

Today Mr. Dover's bow tie is light green with turkeys covering it. It makes me wonder if there's a place like the Brownsville Slaughter Grounds for turkeys, and then that makes me never want to eat Thanksgiving dinner again.

When I get home from school, I take the ninja costume out of my closet. I pull it out of the plastic bag, unfold it, and shake it out. It's in pretty good shape for not having breathed in two years.

Back then Mom took me to Dan's Sporting Goods the night before Halloween, and that's when I found the ninja costume on the sale rack. It was half off, so Mom didn't give it a second thought. Most kids don't buy their Halloween costumes at a sporting goods store, especially one like Dan's, where everything is last year's model or covered in dust. But when your mom is a janitor—even the head janitor—going to a nice costume shop is not an option, because everything there is, according to Mom, "priced for royalty."

During the drive home from Dan's, Mom said, "You can be a ninja next year too."

There was no way I was being the same thing for Halloween two years in a row. So last year I went as an ornithologist. I made the costume from Dad's old birding gear and clothes. A lot of people at school didn't know what I was—even with binoculars hanging around my neck—so I put a name tag on my khaki shirt with "Ornithologist" on it. And then most of the kids couldn't read the name tag because the word was too long. And if they could read it, they didn't know what it meant.

The best thing about my ninja costume is that it's all one piece. This way I don't have to wear a belt or worry about my pants falling down. This mission might involve a lot of army crawling, climbing, and unusual poses, so I have to dress appropriately.

I unzip the costume and put my legs in first. I pull the upper body part over my shoulders and stick my arms through. Then I zip up the front. Now that I think about it, the costume looks like an outfit babies sleep in, only it's all black. It used to be baggy in places, but now the leg parts only come down to my mid-shins. But it'll have to work. Wearing all black is what ninjas and spies do. In movies they find a way to capture their targets, and in the end they always win.

If my plan goes like it should, that'll be me, riding my Predator off into the sunset.

Dad would slap me on the back and be proud. Then he'd say, "Now get your butt off that bike and get out there and find that golden eagle before it kicks the bucket."

Dad had his own way with words.

I stand in front of the mirror in my room. The

costume's arms are way too short, and it's too tight across the chest. If I move suddenly, there's a good chance I'll rip right through it. But there's no turning back. It's the ninja costume or bust. My Predator won't last much longer in Mouton's hands.

I turn around and check out the design on the back of the ninja costume: a bald eagle holding an American flag in its beak.

On Halloween I also wore a fourteen-inch leather glove to represent my partner in crime, my ninja eagle, who just happened to be out on a secret mission all day and night.

In the costume's plastic bag is a small tube of black makeup. I twist the cap off and smell it, like smelling the makeup is really going to determine if it's still okay to use or not. I squeeze out a drop and rub it between my finger and thumb. After deciding it's still good, I sit down at my desk and paint a black mask on my face, just like the northern cardinal's from Gabriela's front yard.

I have some time to kill before meeting up with Gabriela, so I sharpen a pencil and sketch the ruby-throated hummingbird from Gabriela's backyard. Hummingbirds are easy to draw. They're all beaks. Long and pointed.

Bird: Ruby-throated hummingbird

Location: Gabriela's backyard

Note: Seeing so many hummingbirds in one place
is unusual.

Dad: I remember when you taught me how to
listen for hummingbirds.

You said they sound like electricity. Well, I'm
hoping to spark a new friendship.

I hope you've made some friends in your new
habitat.

If not, you should think about putting yourself
out there.

At Gabriela's house I ring the doorbell. This time I have
a decent enough reason to be standing on her porch. She
can't roll her eyes and say, "What brings you here again?"

I wait for her to answer. The night air is cool, but the
ninja costume is so tight that it's trapping my body heat.
Sweat drips down my back, inside my costume.

"Eddie? Is that you?"

"Yeah, it's me."

"You look so scared."

"You mean 'scary'?"

"Yes, that is what I mean." Gabriela looks at her
watch. "You are early."

"I was bored. Mom's working late again. She says it's easier to clean the school when all the kids are gone. I didn't have anyone else to bug."

"Did you have a square meal?"

"Uh, yeah. Leftovers." The truth is, I haven't eaten a thing since lunch. Chicken Patty Tuesday, on Friday. I inhaled everything on my tray except the patty. I picked up the sandwich, took one look at the deep-fried shell, and dropped the whole thing onto my tray. All I could think about was Jeb, the chicken murderer, tossing chicken heads into a bucket.

Gabriela dabs her mouth with a napkin. She and Papa must be in the middle of dinner. "Meet me at the bus stop in ten minutes."

"Ten? I'm roasting in this outfit."

"I will hurry and make it five minutes. Then you will eat your words."

She shuts the door and disappears inside the house. "Square meal"? "Eat your words"? Gabriela is really getting the hang of the harder parts of English.

I leave Gabriela's house and wait at the bus stop. My costume sticks to my back, and black makeup drips from my face.

A pair of square headlights comes rolling toward me. While holding on to the stop sign pole, I swing away from the headlights, hiding my face. If I saw a person wearing all black with a cardinal mask painted on his face, I'd call the police, so I'm not taking any chances.

The car slows down. The brakes squeal louder than my school bus. Out of all the cars in West Plains, there's only one car that makes a sound like that.

Hoopty.

"Eddie? Is that you?" Mom says through the open window.

I keep quiet, hoping she thinks I'm a juvenile delinquent roaming the streets and then drives away. But she's not buying it.

"Eddie. What are you doing out here? And why are you dressed in your spy costume?"

"It's Ninja Bird. Remember?"

The driver's door creaks open. She gets out, cigarette in hand, and stares me up and down. "What's with the outfit? Are you wearing makeup? You must be burning up underneath all that."

"I am." I pull the costume away from my body, letting my skin breathe.

"Then why are you wearing it? Someone's going to mistake you for a burglar and call the police."

"I'm looking for the golden eagle, Mom."

"Oh, Eddie."

"Dad promised that it would come back."

"And you think it's going to come back *tonight*?"

"I don't know when it's coming back, but the more I'm out here, the better my chances of seeing it."

Mom inhales from her cigarette and thinks about it.

"Fine. But you be careful over there at Miss Dorothy's. And stay away from that pond."

She walks back to her car. She drives away, honking twice, and Hoopty's single taillight disappears down the road.

Gabriela walks up next to me. "I'm ready."

I push down the legs of my costume. "Let's go."

Over and Out

Mouton's house is about a quarter mile down the road from mine. It's a small black house that sits in a cluster of oak trees.

Just like the house, the front yard is small. The grass is long and stringy and hasn't been mowed in months. The dull porch light shines down on a brown couch. Dad always said that a house with a couch on the front porch is a house without manners. I don't really know what he meant by that, but Mouton's house must fall into this category.

"Here, take this." I hold out a Donald Duck walkie-talkie. "I changed the batteries. Should be as good as new."

Gabriela takes the walkie-talkie. She looks at it like it's from another planet. "'As good as new'? Is that another phrase I should know?"

"Yes. Now, don't touch the volume button. I preset it so it's not too loud."

"How do I work this talkie-walkie?" She pulls on the antenna.

"Walkie. Talkie. Press the button and talk into this part." I tap the end of the walkie-talkie, the part you speak into.

"I should try it one time."

"Okay, but make it quick."

She presses the button, holding the walkie up to her mouth. "Chirp, chirp. Chirp, chirp."

"What was that?"

"That is what I will say if there is trouble. I thought you would like it."

"I do like it. It's just not something spies would say. They say things like 'over' and 'roger that,' and they have code names like Ringo and Goose and Foxhound."

"Fine. Then I will be Ruby. For ruby-throated hummingbird."

"I'll be golden eagle, but you can just call me Eagle."

Ruby and Eagle. A perfect team.

Now we have to prove that we're worthy of having call signs.

In spy movies only the major characters have code names, the guys with a lot of skills who can fight and shoot and withstand freezing cold water and run through fires without getting burned. Mouton can throw whatever he wants at me. Dog poop. Poison arrows. Woodpecker pens. I'm ready for anything. Nothing's going to stop me from getting my bike.

Gabriela takes her position in the front yard, behind the oak tree. Gabriela is the ideal lookout. She can focus for a long time, way longer than me, and she has 20/20 vision.

I crouch and creep along the driveway. The closer I get to the backyard, the faster my heart races. I was prepared to be nervous, but not like this. This feels more like a panic attack. At least what I imagine a panic attack feeling like.

I stop in the part of the driveway closest to the house and squat behind a rusty station wagon. I whisper into the walkie-talkie, "Ruby, is it all clear? Over."

The walkie crackles, so I turn down the volume. I thought the low setting would be quiet enough. But tonight is especially still. Even the songbirds have turned in for the night.

Gabriela's voice comes over the walkie. "If 'all clear' means everything is okay, then yes, it is all clear. Should I say 'over' now?"

"Yes. Over."

"Okay, Eagle. Over."

From where I'm squatting, the brown couch looks worse than I thought. Worn cushions. Rips. Holes. Burn marks. It's a mess.

I press the walkie button. "Ruby, I'm heading toward the backyard. Over."

"*Boa sorte*, Eagle," Gabriela says. "That means 'good luck.' Over."

From behind the oak tree Gabriela gives me a thumbs-up. "One more thing, Eddie. I mean, Eagle. Leave no stone unturned. Chapter seven. Over."

I stuff the walkie into my cross pouch. Then I creep stealthily around the side of the house toward the backyard.

The backyard is bigger than the front but still small enough for me to see with my mini flashlight. I point the flashlight through the chain-link fence, scanning one section of the yard at a time.

There's a ton of stuff back there. Most of it looks like

circus junk. There's an old tire. A garden gnome. Two pogo sticks. A statue of cupid shooting an arrow. And a bicycle with a huge front wheel and a tiny back wheel. But there's no sign of my bike.

I pull out the walkie and whisper into it. "Ruby, how's it look out there? Over."

No response.

"Ruby? Are you there? Over."

Still no response.

I shine the light close to the back of the house.

There it is.

My bike.

"Ruby. Target in sight. I found it." I try to keep my voice low, but it's hard, knowing that my bike is actually safe. Part of me wasn't sure. Part of me thought it might've been destroyed, strewn over the yard in pieces, or worse—sold—gone forever.

I shine the light onto my bike again to make sure it's not an illusion. Then I pull myself together. Spies can't let their emotions get in their way, even if they have strong feelings for the target.

Gabriela's voice crackles through the walkie. "I'm here, Eagle. Sorry, I could not hold it anymore. I had to use the bathroom. Over."

"Ruby!" I whisper. "You can't leave your post. What if someone leaves or comes home? I'm the recon specialist. You're the lookout. It's your job to inform me if anything changes. Don't leave your post again. Over."

"Okay, okay."

I hold out the mini flashlight, shining it on my bike. "Let's try this again. Any changes to report from the front yard? Over."

"No. All clear, Eagle."

"Then I'm going in."

"Okay, Eddie. I mean, Eagle. Operation Ninja Bird is a go. Over."

"Signing off until target is secure. Over and out."

The Rescue Mission

I unzip the cross pouch and stash the walkie, adjusting the pouch so it's not in my way. I stream the flashlight over my bike. From where I'm crouched it's hard to tell if there's any damage. After seeing the torn-up couch on the front porch, I'm prepared for the worst.

A light from inside the house turns on and comes flooding into the yard. There are no curtains or blinds on the windows, so I have to be cautious. Knocking over the garden gnome or tripping over a pogo stick could lead to failure, and Operation Ninja Bird cannot end in failure.

Soar

I climb the chainlink fence, sticking my shoes inside the gaps and pulling myself up. I plant one foot on the top bar and leap over the fence. I land quietly in the grass.

Stepping around a pogo stick, I slide around the cupid statue, which is bigger than it looked from the side yard.

I run the flashlight along my bike to check its condition. Nicks and scratches cover the frame. The seat stem is loose, and the seat cover is coming off. The handlebars are wobbly, the grips are torn, and the tires—oh, the tires—they're completely flat.

The bedroom light is still on. I wonder if it's Mouton's bedroom or his parents' room. I'm better off not finding out.

I pick up my bike with both hands and walk toward the fence. After three seconds I set it down and catch my breath. Then I use all my strength to lift it over the fence.

Suddenly the back porch light turns on, lighting up the whole backyard.

I drop to the ground, flat on my stomach. I stay as low as possible. The same words keep replaying in my head—spies do NOT get caught—like they're scrolling across a sign in my brain.

My bike lies on the other side of the fence, free at last. But now I'm lying in Mouton's backyard, waiting for Mouton to shine a light in my face and sit on me.

I keep my eyes on the back windows, checking for signs of life. There's a sudden movement in the bedroom.

It's Mouton.

He's facing the wall, his back to me and the window. He's wearing an apron, tied in a knot. Because his back is to me, it's hard to tell what he's doing.

The sight of Mouton in an apron makes me curious. I can't help it. I should hop the fence and walk my bike into the night, with Gabriela walking next to me. I know that's what I should do.

But I have to find out why Mouton is wearing an apron.

I crawl toward the bedroom window, my chest sliding over the wet grass. When I get to a tall patch, I get a face full of weeds and spit them out. I scoot past a second garden gnome, but this one has a missing nose.

I keep crawling.

The bicycle with the huge wheel and tiny wheel looms over me.

When I make it to the window, I rise up into a crouch and peek over the windowsill, into Mouton's bedroom.

Large canvas paintings cover the place. They're everywhere. Propped up on shelves, hanging on walls, stacked in corners. There are even paintings leaning against other paintings.

There's one painting of a little boy sitting alone on a park bench. There's another painting of a multicolored bow tie, which looks like something Mr. Dover would wear. In the corner sits a half-finished painting of two little boys playing in a sandbox.

Mouton takes a step back from his easel to admire the painting he's been working on.

It's a hawk gliding through the air.

It's hard to tell from the window, but it looks like a Cooper's hawk. The wings, body, head, and beak are exactly proportioned. The background—the blue sky and rolling hills—looks like a scene on a postcard. Everything about the painting, especially the hawk, is detailed and accurate and real.

And then I notice something else about the painting. The hawk has one eye.

Mouton isn't painting some random hawk.

He's painting Coop!

All this time, I thought Mouton was just an overgrown ogre who couldn't control what came out of his mouth. But there's a whole other side to him. Who knew that he's probably the best artist in our entire school?

But wait, how does Mouton know about Coop?

Somewhat confused, I drop to my hands and knees and crawl toward the fence. Sliding over the wet grass, I move past the garden gnome. Just as I'm about to reach the fence and my bike, my knee lands on something sharp.

I open my mouth, but stop myself from screaming.

I roll over, holding my knee. The pain shoots from my knee to every part of me.

I find the piece of whatever-attacked-my-kneecap and hold it up against the moonlight. It's a rough piece of broken statue. With nostrils.

The garden gnome's nose.

I stash the nose in my cross pouch. I'm keeping it for remembrance. If I get out of here alive, I'll rub that nose every once in a while to remember what it's like to be a hero.

The bedroom light flicks off.

I hobble up to both feet, throw my good leg over the fence, and fall to the other side. I lift my bike, stand it upright, and hop onto the seat. Pedaling through the grass, I fight through the pain, my good leg doing most of the work. Finally I hit the driveway, which slopes downward, so I give my injured knee a break.

In the front yard Gabriela peeks out from behind the oak tree.

"Come on!" I wave her toward me.

She hops onto the handlebars, just as I had planned, and we bounce away on two flat tires. My good leg does the hard pedaling—but it's almost impossible because the tires have no air in them—while the injured leg just hangs there.

Gabriela holds on to the handlebars tightly. We ride away into the night, away from Mouton's house, away from trouble.

Mouton
Strikes Back

We're halfway down the street, rolling along on two flat tires, when something *tinks* off my bike spokes. I slow my pedaling and look behind us.

Mouton is standing under a streetlight, still dressed in his apron. He's aiming a slingshot at us!

"Go, go, go!" Gabriela shouts from atop the handlebars.

I pedal faster, harder, but my good leg can only do so much. Then a sting takes my breath away, like a syringe pricking my back.

"I've been hit!" I yell.

"What?"

"He hit me in the back!"

It suddenly hurts to talk. It feels like Mouton shot me with a dry ice arrow and froze my skin. The world suddenly turns cloudy. Everything slows down, like it's in superslow motion. Even my hearing is muffled, like I'm swimming underwater. Streaks of fuzzy orange light shoot down from the streetlights. My legs become heavy, and it takes all my effort to keep pedaling.

I blink twice to clear my head, hoping my vision and hearing will go back to normal before I lose control of my bike and dump Gabriela into the street.

"Keep pedaling," Gabriela says. "We are getting closer to my house."

Two more objects ricochet off the pavement next to my bike.

Mouton calls after us. "I'm going to get you, Bird Nerd!"

And then we hear "Eddie-shovel-truck! Eddie-shovel-truck! Eddie . . ." until we leave his words behind and make it safely out of slingshot distance.

At Gabriela's house, under the bathroom light, she examines my back.

"Ahhh." I clench my teeth and wince but try to stay strong. After all, who wants to be friends with a wimp? "What did he hit me with?" I make a seriously tough face.

"I am not sure," Gabriela says. "There is nothing there. Only a large red spot."

Something falls out of my Ninja Bird costume and rolls across the bathroom floor. Gabriela bends down and holds the object up to the light.

"What is it?" I ask her, before the round object comes into focus.

"I think it is a blue piece of chewing gum."

"Mouton shot me with a gumball."

Gabriela places an ice pack over the red welt on my back. "You are luck. This could have been much worse."

"You mean 'lucky.'"

Gabriela presses harder on the ice pack.

"Ouch! Take it easy."

"I knew you would be injured during this mission. Night air is bad air."

"Where did you hear that? Let me guess, *The Phantom Tollbooth*?"

"That is right, Eddie. I am learning more English phrases from Milo and his dog than I am learning at school."

"Have you made it to the part in the book when they go to the—"

"Eddie! Do not ruin the story for me!"

She adjusts the ice pack on my red welt.

"You should see Mouton's room," I say, remembering what I saw at Mouton's house. "It's covered in all these paintings that look real. I can't believe he can paint like that."

"I am not surprised."

"Really? How can you not be surprised?"

"Everyone has a talent. Mouton cannot control what comes out of his mouth, but he can control what he puts on a white canvas."

I look at my back in the mirror. "You know, when you say it like that, it sort of makes sense."

"Maybe he can help you with your project," she says, holding the ice pack steady.

"Maybe." I shrug. And that's when I realize that if I want to win the blue ribbon, I'll first have to win Mouton. That's going to be difficult. I have a better chance of finding a dodo than convincing Mouton to work on our project.

"Thanks for doing this," I say to Gabriela. "I mean, for being the lookout. It means a lot to me."

"I will be your lookout anytime. This is what friends are for."

Wow, I really *am* lucky.

I have my bike.

I have a friend.

Somehow I found a way to get two birds with one mission.

Me and You,
You and Me

When I get home from Gabriela's house, I lift up on the garage door handle. The door rolls up and rattles open. Mom leaves the garage door unlocked for me because she knows I'll need to put my bike away for the night.

I walk my bike inside the garage and put the kickstand down. I roll the garage door down and lock it tight. Then I look at my bike one last time—the crooked handlebars, ripped up seat, loose hand brakes, flat tires.

If my dad saw my bike now, he'd be disappointed in me. He'd give me advice, like he did when I lost my first pair of binoculars when I was five years old.

"You have to protect the meaningful things in your life," he told me. "You can't let other people destroy what's important to you. It could be something as simple as a pair of binoculars or a stuffed animal. The point is, if it's important enough to make you feel empty inside when it's gone, it's important enough to protect with all your heart."

I walk through the door that leads from the garage into our house.

Mom meets me at the door, with watery eyes and her hands on her hips. She is pretty much waiting to yell at me.

"Eddie, it's almost ten o'clock. Where have you been?"

I say nothing. I know I'm in big trouble already, so I don't want to lie about spying at Mouton's house when I was supposed to be at Miss Dorothy's place. It feels better just to keep quiet.

"I had no idea what happened to you," she says. "For all I knew, you were at the bottom of Miss Dorothy's pond. I was about to call the police!"

I avoid eye contact and walk toward my room.

Mom grabs my arm, turns me toward her, and looks me in the eye.

"Look at me when I'm talking to you. I seriously thought you could be dead. Do you understand what that means?"

My bottom lip begins to tremble, just like it did at Gabriela's house when I was telling her about Dad flying away for good.

The truth is, I feel guilty for staying out two hours past curfew, and for making Mom worry so much. Mom has enough to worry about, like how to pay bills and how to put food on the table. She doesn't need me stressing her out even more.

I put my head down and lean toward her. I bury my forehead in her shoulder.

She hugs me and rubs my back. Even though she can't always give me what I want, Mom always knows what I need most. And right now I need her.

"I'm sorry for yelling at you," she says. "I've already lost one piece of this family. I'm not going to lose another."

She takes hold of my shoulders and looks me in the eye again.

"Me and you. You and me. This is all we've got, Eddie. We have to protect each other forever. You understand that?"

I can barely move, because I feel horrible about making my mom worry so much. I understand everything she's saying, but if I open my mouth to talk right now, I might cry and never be able to stop.

So I nod quietly.

Then I imagine my tears flooding our house and washing away all the bad memories of Dad being sick.

Predator = Good, Prey = Bad

On Monday morning at school I open my locker and take out my science book. The welt on my back hurts like crazy. I still can't believe Mouton used a slingshot to peg me with a gumball. I can believe he took aim at me, but it's hard to imagine that he actually hit his target, which was MY BACK.

"You got your Predator, but you're still my prey." Mouton stands across the hall from me, at his locker, his arms crossed.

"I told you I'd get my bike."

"You came on my property without permission. This means war."

"Mouton, if you're going to keep stolen property in your backyard, then you should pay more attention to it. You must've been too busy painting."

He throws his arms down at his sides. "Hey, you weren't supposed to see that!"

"Too late." I stuff my science book into my backpack. "I saw everything."

Mouton's face and neck turn red. He pulls out his woodpecker pen from his pocket. He clicks it repeatedly.

Open-closed-open-closed-open-closed.

Faster and faster.

Until his hand shakes out of control.

"Woodpecker-woodpecker-woodpecker! Yip!"

I can tell he's trying to control what comes out of his mouth, but he can't help it. Part of me wants to take his woodpecker pen and stomp on it because he ruined my bike. The other part of me feels sorry for him, because there are times when he has no idea what he's going to say next. I can't imagine what that must feel like on the inside. He must be full of worry all the time, like Mom worrying about me. Except Mouton's worry never goes away. He was born that way, and he can't get rid of it.

"You're a good artist, Mouton, I'll give you that," I

say. "But that doesn't change what you did to my bike."

Mouton leans against the lockers, holding the pen at his side, still clicking it open and closed. "Yip-yip." He looks down at the floor.

I can tell by his slumped shoulders and turned-down face that he's nervous. Maybe he's searching for ways to stop the worry.

I know a lot about worry from when Dad was sick. I wouldn't wish that kind of feeling on my worst enemy, including Mouton.

For the whole week, during science class we type up content for our poster boards. On the day of the symposium, each group displays a tri-fold poster board on their table. On the board we're supposed to have six categories about our project:

Title.

Hypothesis.

Purpose.

Materials.

Evidence.

Conclusion.

The display board is a big part of our grade, so the quality of our content is really important.

Gabriela and Trixie sit in the far corner of the classroom. Their computer screen lights up Trixie's orange hair, making it glow.

Mr. Dover walks around the room, checking on the progress of each group. Today he's wearing a black bow tie. It has two white eyes and two fangs. It's supposed to be a bat, but it looks more like a Halloween project I made in kindergarten.

"You should be able to finish your materials list today," Mr. Dover says to the class. "And both partners should be contributing equally."

Gabriela and Trixie's computer screen is all fancy and bright and colorful, which means they must be making progress.

Our screen is white, because it's blank.

Mouton drums his woodpecker pen on the table. "Let me type," he complains. "You never let me do anything."

I pause, deciding how much responsibility to give Mouton. Then I remember the look on his face at the lockers when he was trying to control his vocal tics. Maybe if he's able to focus his energy on our project, his worry will go away.

"He has a point." Mr. Dover stands behind me.

Soar

"You're partners, and you need to work together. You only have a week until the symposium."

After Mr. Dover walks away, I get up and let Mouton sit at the computer. Before he starts typing, he shoves his pen into his pocket and pats his pocket three times.

Gabriela walks past me, touching my shoulder. "Time flies when you are having fun. Over."

She walks toward the printer to get a piece of paper.

Trixie's glowing orange hair blocks their computer screen. If I could catch a glimpse of their screen, I might be able to figure out what their project is about. It'd be helpful to know what the competition is up to, since Gabriela won't tell me.

Mouton pecks at the keyboard, one letter at a time.

"There. Finished."

He leans back in his chair, admiring what he has typed on the screen. Everything is in size forty-eight font.

Materials
1. poster
B. tape
3. Woodpecker pens (one from every state)
4. $
5. gumballs

I sigh and bury my face in my hands. I finally look up. "Are you serious, Mouton? What is this?"

"It's our materials list."

"That's not the project Mr. Dover approved. Besides, you shooting me with a gumball has nothing to do with the science symposium or this class or anything else."

Mouton just sits there, looking at the screen. He refuses to talk.

I can't help but wonder if he's being stubborn or if he's pushing the worry down inside him and fighting the urge to say something he doesn't mean to say.

"How about we work on the materials list together?" I suggest. "We can start by making the font smaller."

Mouton looks at me, then at the computer screen. "Yip-yip."

I guess that's his way of saying yes.

So for the rest of class, we work on the materials list together. It takes some working and reworking, and some major compromising, but we eventually get the hang of working together. By the end of class, Mouton becomes an expert in fonts, and he actually chooses some neat designs. He even draws a bird's nest on the computer with the mouse, and it looks totally real.

"Mouton! That's awesome!" I say. "How'd you do that?"

Mouton saves the document on the screen. "I think it needs more twigs."

"No, no. It looks great the way it is."

Mr. Dover doesn't bother interrupting us. He's the kind of teacher who lets students work things out by themselves. Well, I have news for Mr. Dover. Mouton and I are *finally* working things out and moving in the right direction on our project.

But besides drawing and choosing neat fonts, there's nothing else Mouton has shown interest in. Nothing.

Wait a second!

Mouton is an artist!

Birds.

Art.

Birds.

Art.

Yes!

That's it!

Mouton can paint the golden eagle!

Sandy—
Mr. Fix-It

West Plains doesn't have much of a down-town. But what it doesn't have in fancy buildings it makes up for in small shops. Mom calls them nugget shops, because she says there is at least one good deal with her name on it—a golden nugget—in each shop. Dad said most of the shops are worthless. He called them junk shops.

The main shops are Clocks N Things, Al's Antiques, Teddy's Toy Tractors, and Sigfried's Dollar Depot. A block down the road from all those shops sits Pumps, the only gas station in town, and further down from that is a garage with two police cars and one fire truck.

Soar

Dad always called West Plains a one-horse town. It sounds like one of those phrases Gabriela is always saying.

On Saturday afternoon I walk my dying bike past the Freeze Queen on my way to Jetz Skating Rink.

The Freeze Queen is a one-story white building with huge windows outlined in pink neon lights. The sign out front has more pink lights that outline a vanilla ice cream cone, with a queen's crown on top of it. The Freeze Queen is mostly known for ice cream, but a lot of people, like Mom and me, go there for the Buck Burgers.

My poor, poor bike. The frame squeaks, the handlebars aren't aligned properly, the pedals and seat are loose, and the tires are in sad shape.

The symposium is coming soon, and I have a lot of work to do. But I can't roll around town on a broken bike. There's only one person who can put my Predator back together again.

Sandy.

Dad said Sandy could build a house out of paper that would stand up to a tornado. Just like the golden eagle, Dad wouldn't lie about something like that.

Jetz Skating Rink sits between the end of Main

Street's junk shops and Pumps Gas Station. It's not at the end of town, but close to it. A lot of kids come to Jetz on Saturday nights. There's music, arcade games, popcorn, pizza. And if you get bored, there's always roller-skating. If nothing else, it's a place to hang out, away from your parents. It's only two bucks to get in, plus money to rent skates.

Sandy owns and manages the place, but he never makes a dime, because he doesn't charge enough for food or skate rentals. Prices were about the same when Dad was a kid. But that's Sandy for you. He doesn't care about money. That's why he drives a bus for almost nothing and lives in his camper close to school.

Another thing about Sandy is that he always comes to the symposium. He won the blue ribbon, but that was when there were about twenty kids in seventh grade, so it wasn't a big deal back then like it is today.

When I open the front door to Jetz Skating Rink, the welcome bell rings. I walk my bike down the ramp. The whole place is covered in carpet that's not really carpet but just a padless floor covering. When you fall while roller-skating, it hurts pretty bad. Mom says this type of carpet is easy to clean and that's why Sandy installed it.

Sandy moves around behind the rental counter, spraying the inside of skates with air freshener.

I roll my bike close to the counter and stop. "Aerosol is bad for the environment," I tell him.

Sandy ignores me. He grabs another pair of skates. Size six, with red-and-white checkered laces and a loose wheel. He shoves the aerosol can inside the skates and sprays. I wore that same pair in fourth grade, the night I skated with Camilla Caflisch. The night I threw watered-down Coke at Mouton because he wouldn't stop calling me Fish Boy in front of her. The night I had to say good-bye to my best friend, because the next day Camilla left for Switzerland and never came back.

"Sue me," Sandy says, without looking up.

He sets the skates aside and takes another pair. Size eight, blue-and-green laces, three red wheels and one white, probably a wheel that Sandy had to replace. That pair gives me blisters on my heels. "You ride that bike to the underworld and back?" he asks.

"That's why I'm here. You can fix anything. And you told me to find you if I needed something. Well, I need something."

Sandy sprays the eights and sets them on the rack. He comes out from behind the counter and takes a long look at my bike. He takes the handlebar and leans the frame away from us so he can see it better in the overhead lights.

"Careful," I say. "The whole frame is loose."

He laughs under his breath. "You got more problems than loose." He sets my bike on its kickstand and walks behind the counter. He slurps from a Styrofoam cup covered in greasy fingerprints.

"Does that mean you'll fix it?" I ask him.

Sandy turns his back and walks away. Just when I think he's ignoring me, he motions for me to follow him. Relieved, I take a deep breath, guiding my bike with one hand on the handlebars, the other hand on the seat.

The back part of Jetz Skating Rink is a storage area, but Sandy uses it more as a garage. Tools cover the walls and fill every corner. Hammers, saws, levels, clamps, wrenches. A can of Roller Shine hangs above a workbench, and extra wooden planks lean against a storage cabinet. The planks must be extra pieces for the skating rink floor.

Sandy reaches up and yanks a long chain hanging from the ceiling. A light bulb flicks on. Under the light my bike looks like it belongs in a junkyard.

Sandy bends down and checks out the front wheel where it attaches to the bike frame. He pulls a wrench from his toolbox and cranks the screw in the middle of the wheel a few times.

"Is that really going to work?" I ask him.

Sandy cranks the screw one last time. He doesn't bother looking up.

"Sorry," I say. "I'll shut up."

I don't blame Sandy for being annoyed. He's used to working in silence. No one's ever here during the day. But there's one question I have to ask him.

"Sandy, I really need to ask you something."

He looks up at me, showing me his toothless grin. "What is it, Eddie?"

I look at my bike, remembering that night at Dan's Sporting Goods and how proud my dad was for buying it. He wanted me to ride it so badly that when we got home, he backed Hoopty into the driveway and lit up our street with the headlights so I could see where I was going.

I look at Sandy, wondering if he'd tell me the truth.

"Was my dad a liar?" I ask him.

Sandy takes a deep breath. He walks around to the back wheel and begins tightening the screw in the middle.

"A liar, huh?" he says, thinking about it. "Your daddy was the biggest liar that ever saw a bird."

My New and Improved Bike

It takes a moment for Sandy's words to sink in. I can't tell if he's serious or joking. I can only hope he's heading toward a funny story about Dad lying once—only once—about something other than birds.

My response barely makes it out. "Really?"

"Sure. Your dad lied to me all the time. He'd say the food he brought me was just some leftovers from your mom's kitchen. Half the time he left the price tag on it."

It's true. On our way home from birding on some nights, Dad would stop at the store and come out with a brown bag with hot food inside.

"What's Sandy going to eat tonight?" I'd ask, and Dad would say, "He's going to eat good."

"Did he lie about anything else?"

"Why you asking me, Eddie? Did someone call your dad a liar? If so, you should tell 'em to stop stickin' their nose where it don't belong."

I shrug. "It's nothing like that. It's okay."

"'Okay,' someone called your dad a liar, or 'Okay,' you'll tell 'em to sniff elsewhere? Which is it?"

"Both, I guess."

Sandy chuckles, showing his gap-filled smile. He takes a smaller wrench from his toolbox.

"Hold the handlebars steady," he orders.

I straddle the front tire, facing my bike, holding the handlebars in place. Sandy begins tightening the screw that connects the handlebars to the frame. "Your dad was a tasteful liar. He only lied when the situation called for it. He lied about meaningless things, like bringing me food. He didn't lie about things that mattered."

"Did he ever tell you about the golden eagle?"

"The golden eagle," Sandy says, remembering out loud. "Yeah, I knew about it." He yanks on the wrench. "Give those handlebars a tug."

I pull up on the handlebars. They won't budge. They're even tighter and sturdier than before.

"Seems good to me. Thanks."

"We're not done yet." He pulls a tool from his back pocket and begins removing one of the links in the greasy chain. After he removes the link, he takes the chain off and drops it into a bucket filled with a blue cleaning solution—just like the cleaner Mom uses at school. The water turns from blue to black, I'm guessing from all the grease on the chain. Now it looks like a bucket of water from Miss Dorothy's pond.

"Do you think my dad lied about the golden eagle?"

"Did he have a reason to?" Sandy lifts the chain out of the bucket. Black water drips from it. But under the light the chain sparkles like it did on the day I rolled my bike toward the cashier at Dan's Sporting Goods.

Sandy lays the chain on a towel. "Can't let the chain sit in water for too long or it'll rust."

"I don't think Dad had a reason to lie." I try to keep the conversation going.

"Hold the handlebars again."

I straddle the front wheel, holding the handlebars steady. With both hands Sandy twists the seat back and forth until it pops out of the frame. Then he puts my bike seat in a different bucket—one that's filled with what looks like plain water. "Give it a few minutes. That stuff will clean mud off a hog."

I decide to go for it. "Sandy, do you think the golden eagle is real? Do you think he actually saw it?"

Sandy sprays a rag with clear liquid and begins wiping down the silver frame. My bike begins to turn into a brand-new mode of transportation. It's still my Predator, but it's better than the Predator I've known for the last year.

"If the golden eagle is real, I wanna see it," he says. "And if it's phony, I don't wanna know. Uncertainties make life more interesting."

"What do you mean?"

"On Saturday nights I never know how many kids are gonna walk through that door. Could be ten. Twenty. Thirty on a good night. If it were always the same number, and the same kids, I'd get bored of this place real quick. I'll be here on Saturday night, that much is certain. But there's also the unexpected. Like the night you threw soda in Mouton's face. I laughed myself to sleep thinking about that."

"You did?" I suddenly feel horrible about that night. Mouton was annoying me and pushed me to the limit, but I could've reacted differently.

The soda stain—a dark blotchy outline that looks like Texas—still covers the carpet where you enter the roller rink.

Sandy finishes cleaning my bike frame and tosses the rag onto his work counter. The light from overhead shimmers off the crossbar that holds the seat in place.

"Take this here bike," Sandy says. "I'm doing my best to fix it up nice for you, but I don't know what's going to happen once you start riding it. It could fall apart and turn you sideways into a ditch. Or it could hold sturdy until you outgrow it. Uncertainties. They're all around us, but you don't realize it because they're quiet. They're not like tragedies or maladies. Those things hit you over the head. Uncertainties lurk. They can haunt you or surprise you. Guess it depends on what you expected in the first place."

I've never heard Sandy talk like this.

He sounds like Mr. Dover during one of his stories about his property. But Sandy's words make a lot more sense, in a real-life kind of way.

Buck Burger
Betrayal

Sandy even reupholsters the seat for me. By the way he checks everything twice, you'd think he was fixing the president's bike. I ask Sandy for a spool of string for my symposium project, and he gives it to me.

On my way out of Jetz Skating Rink, he says, "I never asked you, what happened to your bike?"

I swing the door open, and the welcome bell rings, only this time it's the good-bye bell. I stand in the open doorway, holding on to my bike. The smells of Indiana fall and Roller Shine hit me at once.

Sandy says "Maybe some other time" and waves me out the door.

I hop onto my Predator, feeling out the new seat cover, and begin pedaling.

The newness and sturdiness of everything takes me back to Dan's Sporting Goods and Dad, standing in the aisle, nodding his head, waiting patiently for me to pick out my birthday present. I still don't know where he got the money for it.

I tuck the spool of string under my shirt and pedal harder. I coast over to the Freeze Queen, hoping Mom has stopped there on her way home from work. There's a good chance she'll show up here. All the workers know her name, except the high school girl behind the counter who calls her Lizzie instead of Lisa. Mom's too sweet to correct her.

When I get to the Freeze Queen, I hop off my bike and guide it toward the entrance. I'm not leaving it outside again. I've run into Mouton here plenty of times. He always buys a sackful of Buck Burgers and then walks home, holding the sack in one hand, inhaling burgers with the other. That makes me wonder if Mouton has ever painted a Buck Burger. If he has, I bet all the details—the melted cheese, the juicy burger, the smooshed sesame seed bun—look mouthwatering and real enough to eat.

I look through the windows of the Freeze Queen.

Mom is not standing in line. She's not at the soda machine. She's not grabbing a sack of Buck Burgers for dinner. She's nowhere to be found.

But someone I know *is* sitting in a booth.

Gabriela.

And she's not alone.

Chase, the basketball player, sits next to her. He says something, and Gabriela laughs, covering her smile with her hand.

Gabriela looks like a movie star under the booth's lights. She and Chase are sharing a basket of fries and using the same ketchup cup.

I walk my bike through the front door and guide it across the black-and-white checkered floor. I stop in front of Gabriela's booth.

When Gabriela sees me, she smiles and acts like everything is fine. "Hi, Eddie. What are you doing here?"

Chase glances at me, then the bike. "Look, it's Mr. Muscles."

Ignoring Chase, I focus on Gabriela. "I'm looking for my mom. What are *you* doing here?"

Gabriela looks down at the basket of fries and the paper ketchup container. "Chase has to do a country report for his social studies class. He chose Brazil as his country, so I am here to help him get his facts straight."

"Must be nice." I glare at Chase.

"Chase asked to interview me as part of his research," Gabriela says.

"It doesn't look like much research is going on here," I say. "Where's the journal and the pencil? What about the voice recorder?"

"Eddie, we are only having a conversation about my home country. That is all."

Chase reaches out and touches my bike tire. "Bike's looking good there, Wing Man. You should get going, though. There's a lot of baby robins to save before winter."

I glare at him, but all I see are his broad shoulders and muscular arms. "For your information, I conduct real research on my subjects."

"Real research, huh? I haven't heard anything about you doing research, but I heard you like to dress up like a baby ninja."

My heart pounds, my face turns hot. I glare at Gabriela. "You told him about our mission?" How could she do this? Operation Ninja Bird was our special mission, never to be spoken about.

"Eddie, it is not what you think," she says. "I told Chase that your costume was cute. That is all."

"Cute? Is that what you think of me? I'm the cute little boy who lives down the street, who dresses up like a ninja, who chases birds? I thought we were friends."

"Eddie. Please," she says. "You are putting words into my mouth."

"Whatever. In one ear and out the other. Over."

I turn my bike around and head for the exit. The door swings open, and I almost run over Mom.

"Eddie," Mom says. "Where are you going?"

"I'm going home."

"Well, wait for me. I called ahead. I'm getting dinner for us."

Mom looks past me, noticing Gabriela and Chase sitting in the booth. "Ah, I see what's going on here. I'm sorry, sweetie," she whispers.

I put my head down, embarrassed, because I can feel people watching us.

Mom keeps her voice low. "Chase is a good kid. He plays basketball and gets good grades. I can see why Gabriela is friends with him."

"How do you know about his grades?"

"Honor roll, sweetie. You know, the same list you

fell from after—" Mom stops herself midsentence.

I finish it for her. "After Dad flew away. Why can't you just say it? You never talk about him. Face it, he's gone! Gone, gone, gone! Just say it!"

Now *everyone* is watching us. Cooks. Busboys. Chase and Gabriela. People standing in line.

The high school girl behind the counter breaks the silence. "Excuse me, Lizzie." She holds out a white paper sack.

Mom takes the sack from her. "It's Lisa, not Lizzie."

I storm out the exit, rolling my bike next to me. I tuck the spool of string from Sandy under my shirt and hop onto my new seat. Pedaling hard, I take off down the street, leaving Gabriela and Chase and Mom and all those Buck Burgers in the dust.

Before long my eyes fill with tears and my vision goes blurry. It takes everything I have to stay focused on the road in front of me.

Unexpected Visitor

While pedaling home, I think about Gabriela and Chase sitting in the booth, laughing with each other. It was stupid to think that Gabriela and I had a special friendship. But why else would she spend so much time with me?

There's only one place I want to be right now, and that's at Miss Dorothy's—with Coop.

I stop pedaling and coast across my front yard. I lay my bike down near the porch. I open the front door and go inside to gather items for my field research. First I throw my cross pouch over my shoulder, and then I go into my room for my mini flashlight.

My stomach rumbles, so I take a granola bar from the pantry.

I walk into the garage and rummage through some of Dad's dust-covered things until I find what I'm looking for. A green case with a shoulder strap. Dad's night vision binoculars. I sling the strap over my shoulder.

Then I notice Dad's symposium project sitting in the corner. He kept the poster board all these years, because he wanted to show it to me when I made it to seventh grade.

I step over a bumper-stickered suitcase and walk toward the huge three-panel poster, which is covered with photos and captions. I clear the cobwebs, and two daddy longlegs scatter in opposite directions. I turn the poster around and see Dad's name:

JOSEPH WILSON
SEVENTH GRADE

I think about what Dad was like in seventh grade. Did other students make up nicknames for him at school? Did he fight with kids who lived in his neighborhood? Did he have a best friend?

I leave the garage, hop on my bike, and take off,

pedaling through the neighborhood. When I get to Miss Dorothy's house, I walk my bike through the side yard.

The moon is only a crescent shape tonight, but its weak light reflects off my bike's silver frame, thanks to Sandy's polishing.

Coop usually hunts right around dusk, and then disappears for the night to avoid owls and other predators. Coop is old—going on thirteen—but hunting in the early evening can be easier for her, since that's when a lot of small critters come searching for food.

Dad told me that Coop had babies when she was two, just about the time all female hawks do. Ever since then she's been alone. Most raptors don't stay in one territory for this long, but something has kept Coop here. Dad said it was me that's kept her here all this time, but I'm pretty sure he said that to make me feel better, and to forget about him being sick.

Coop should come around soon. She can always sense when I need her most.

I put down the kickstand on my bike and crouch in the cattails near the pond. While waiting for the sky to darken completely, I listen to the twitters and warbles of American goldfinches. Their yellow and black colors are striking, even in the twilight. One of the goldfinches sounds like it's saying, *Po-ta-to-chip, po-ta-to-chip.*

When the sun is down, I take out Dad's night vision binoculars and slip the strap over my head. Everything looks green through the binoculars, but at least I can see what's around me.

For my field research my plan is to set a string-and-twig trap with the string Sandy gave me. Hopefully this will let me catch a small rodent. Then I'll take the rodent and tie it high up in a tree. With the critter meat, I hope to hit the right combination to attract the golden eagle.

I stow the binoculars in the case and get to work on setting the traps. With a few strong branches from nearby trees, and the string, I make two traps, one on each side of the pond. The traps don't kill the rodents. They catch them by the body or leg so they can't get free.

While I'm working on the traps, something stirs in the brush on the other side of the pond.

A large figure comes out from the tall grass and walks toward me. I shut off my flashlight and stay low. Then I pull out Dad's night vision binoculars and take a look.

The Agreement

I t's Mouton. He trudges toward me, through the overgrown brush.

I shine the flashlight right between his eyes. "What are you doing here?"

"Put that thing down," he says. "I can't see."

"First tell me why you're here."

"I'm here to find that bird."

"What bird?"

"The one that lives here."

"You talking about Coop?"

He shrugs. "I don't know. Who's Coop?"

I lower the flashlight, and he walks toward me. When he gets close, I shine the light in his eyes. "You're not allowed to be on Miss Dorothy's land. But how do you know about Coop?"

Mouton shields his eyes from the light. "I've seen a hawk flying in our neighborhood. I decided to follow it, and it came here."

"It's a *her*, not an it." I lower the flashlight.

Mouton looks at my shiny Predator, which stands tall in the moonlight.

I point the flashlight at Mouton's chest. "Don't even think about touching my bike."

A deep, soft hoot comes from a distant tree.

Hoo-h'HOO-hoo-hoo.

"What's that?" Mouton asks.

"It's a great horned owl." I look off into the distance, where the sound came from. I listen closely, but the frogs are the only sound left.

"Does it really have horns?"

"Well, yeah, kind of. They're called ear tufts, but they look like horns."

The owl breaks the silence, like it knows we're talking about it.

Hoo-h'HOO-hoo-hoo.

Mouton looks at my Predator. "Eddie-shovel-truck! Yip!"

My eyes begin to adjust to the darkness. I can see Mouton's white T-shirt, but not the details of his face. "Why do you always say that? I mean, you don't even like me, so why do you always say my name?"

He crosses his arms, looking at the ground. "I don't know. It just comes out. I can't control it."

Sandy was right. Uncertainties make life interesting. But if I could give Mouton my voice for a day, then he'd know what it's like to be in control. He could get rid of his uncertainties and release his worries into the wild.

Coop swoops down and soars over our heads. I point the flashlight at her. Mouton and I flinch and duck at the same time. Coop rises high, covering us like the arms of a sycamore tree. She perches on a branch, staring down at us.

"There you are," I say, holding the flashlight on her.

Mouton moves toward the tree and looks up. He stares at Coop and can't seem to take his eyes off her.

"You know, I thought of a way you can show off your skills," I say to Mouton. I keep the flashlight on Coop, and she keeps looking at us. "A way you can help with our project."

"What is it?"

"Painting."

He shrugs. "Yeah, so?"

"Look," I tell him. "I'm not asking for your help because I feel sorry for you or anything like that. I'm asking because I think you'd do a good job."

Mouton looks at me, crosses his arms. "Why should I help you?"

"Because if we don't work together, we'll fail our project. Then you'll be right back in Mr. Dover's class again next year, listening to his boring stories about his stupid property."

He uncrosses his arms, puts his hands at his sides. "I'm listening."

"Forget about me or Mr. Dover. You should do it for yourself, Mouton. You have a voice, but no one knows about it. You've kept it hidden all these years. Now's your chance to let everyone hear you."

"So what's your plan?"

"I'll do the field study. You paint a golden eagle. At the symposium we'll display your painting next to our materials and research. What do you say?"

Mouton looks up at Coop. She stares down at us like she's waiting for Mouton to answer my question.

Soar

Then, from far away, comes the owl again.

Hoo-h'HOO-hoo-hoo.

"Fine," Mouton says. "I'll do it. But I've never seen a golden eagle. How am I supposed to paint one?"

"You can borrow my field guide." I look up at the stars dotting the black sky, some brighter than others. "Or maybe you'll see a golden eagle soon."

Hopes . . . Shy
Birds . . . Guns

Mouton looks up at Coop. "See you around," he says, and then he walks away, disappearing into the night.

Now that Mouton has agreed to do the painting, our symposium project is on the right track. Order and progress, just like the Brazilian flag hanging in Gabriela's house.

I check my traps one last time. Then I cruise home on my bike.

As I pass Gabriela's house, the northern cardinal's song drifts down from the tall oak tree in her front yard. Part of me wants to stop and give Gabriela a piece of my mind. We were supposed to be friends, but now she's spending time with Chase, and she told him about our secret mission. So much for keeping things between us.

I put my bike away in the garage.

Before going inside the house, I decide to check out Dad's project one more time. I reread all of his research, hoping that it will inspire me.

I remember this one quote Dad used to say every time we went looking for the golden eagle:

"But Hopes are Shy Birds flying at a great distance seldom reached by the best of Guns."

The words from the quote make me think of my own project.

Hopes—of winning the blue ribbon.

Shy Birds—finding the golden eagle.

Guns—proving my shotgun-carrying science teacher wrong.

There's a beige envelope—the same kind Mr. Dover uses to send detention slips to the office— attached to the back of the poster board. I pull the envelope off carefully, but it takes a thin layer of poster board with it.

Sorry, Dad.

I open the envelope and pull out a newspaper article. The paper is thin and yellowish, and the ink is fading. It's a page from the *West Plains Post*.

JOE WILSON WINS SCIENCE SYMPOSIUM
LAMB DOVER TAKES SECOND PLACE

I hold the article in front of me, staring at the words. I feel like going to Mr. Dover's house and asking him why he doesn't like me, and then right when he's about to answer, showing him the newspaper article.

Instead I slip the article back into the beige envelope and seal it. I tuck the envelope under my shirt and go inside the house.

A greasy Freeze Queen sack sits on the kitchen table. I open the fridge, but there's not much in there. A quarter gallon of milk, a half-empty bottle of ketchup, and something wrapped in foil. I take out the orange juice container and drink the last gulp. I pitch the orange juice carton into the recycling can.

The theme song from *One Last Life* blares from the living room.

Mom jingles into the kitchen, holding a cigarette between two fingers. "Use a glass, you barbarian.

Where were you?" She breathes out of her nose, filling the space above the sink with smoke.

"I was at Miss Dorothy's, working on my project."

"I thought so." She scoots the grease-spotted Freeze Queen sack closer to me. "I got our Buck Burgers. Cold cow's better than no cow."

My stomach growls as soon as Mom says "Buck Burgers." I reach into the sack, pull out a burger, unwrap half of it, and take a bite.

Mom stands close to me. I can feel her looking at me. "You okay?"

I talk through a mouthful. "Yeah, I'm fine."

"You sure about that? Do you want to talk about this Gabriela situation?"

"There's no situation, Mom. But thanks."

I walk into my room and shut the door.

The Buck Burger doesn't taste as good as it usually does. I pitch the rest of the burger into the trash can. I bury it underneath a bunch of old bird sketches so Mom doesn't see that I've wasted food.

I pull the beige envelope from underneath my shirt and put it safely in my desk drawer. I open my bird journal to a blank page in the Raptors section and begin sketching the owl from Miss Dorothy's place.

Like Dad told me in second grade after I successfully identified my first American robin call, "Identifying a bird by its call is better than identifying it by sight, because that means you're finally opening your ears and listening to the music."

The owl's beak is short and curved. The head is round, the body full; the ear tufts stick straight up. Owls are easy to draw, but it's hard to make the head the right size compared to the body. I always draw the head too big or too small, and then it turns out looking like a caricature.

I think of owls as silent assassins and guardians of secrets—just like ninjas.

Bird: Great horned owl

Location: Miss Dorothy's place

Note: With Mouton's voice, there is hope for our project.

Dad: Making friends is a tough business. Sometimes I wonder if it's worth the trouble.

I'm trying to listen to the music, but it's hard to hear the words.

I Talk
to Coop

On Monday morning I get up early and get dressed. When I walk into the kitchen, Mom is standing at the sink.

"Where are you going so early?" she asks me. She cracks the window above the sink, her keys clinking together. She strikes a match and lights a cigarette.

I shut the fridge door. "We're out of orange juice."

"Drink water. It's good for you." Mom flicks ashes out the window. She blows smoke out her nose, and it billows in the sink.

"I'm going to Miss Dorothy's." I sling my jacket over

my shoulder, along with my backpack, and head for the front door.

"I better be the first to know when you see that bird."

"Don't worry. When I see it, the whole town will know."

I get my bike from the garage, hop onto it, and pedal down the street.

When I arrive at Miss Dorothy's, the traps are knocked down. One trap even has a squirrel by the leg! The dirty work is out of the way. It's already dead. It had to be either Coop or the great horned owl. Whoever did it saved me time and left the squirrel in decent shape.

Using the leftover string from the trap, I tie the squirrel by the legs and sling it over my back. I climb up the tallest of the trees and tie the dead squirrel to a branch.

Eagles are the most dominant hunters on earth, but while migrating, they can also be serious scavengers. Once I read about a group of ornithologists setting out an eagle buffet like this. Right now, with the science symposium coming up soon, it's my best option.

As I climb down the tree, Coop lands on a branch close to me. She flaps her wings, as if saying, *Good morning*.

"Hey there, Coop. Now listen, you stay away from this squirrel. It's not for you."

She stares at me, and then lets out a loud *cak-cak-cak*,

which is a call that Cooper's hawks use to defend their territory.

I'm not worried about Coop feeling threatened by me. We've known each other forever. But I do get the feeling that she's interested in the squirrel.

"Listen, Coop. I need you to protect this squirrel, okay? I need it for my project at school. I have to find that golden eagle. Now, you let me know if anything happens, okay? I want to hear you loud and clear."

I realize Coop doesn't understand what I'm saying to her, but if there's a chance that birds understand human desperation, then maybe she'll decide to lay off the squirrel. And if I'm really lucky, she'll chase away any vultures.

Coop flaps her wings and flies through the trees, probably looking for a house sparrow or mourning dove for breakfast. Maybe even a northern flicker, because they spend a lot of time on the ground, which makes them easy targets.

I climb down the tree and ride away on my bike. At home I park my bike in the garage and then walk toward the bus stop.

When I get there, Gabriela is standing close to the stop sign. She doesn't look at me, so I pretend to ignore her.

Death Smell

At the bus stop I stand at least twenty feet away from Gabriela. I have nothing to say to her. But every thirty seconds or so, I glance at her, then look away.

Each time I look over at her, she's writing in her notebook. I can't help but wonder what she's writing about.

Mouton walks up and stands close to me. "Morning, Chicken Legs."

"Morning," I say.

When we get on the bus, I stare out the window. I'm sure Gabriela is writing down all the reasons she wants to be friends with Chase instead of me.

Soar

In Mr. Dover's class it's frog dissection week, which explains why the classroom reeks of formaldehyde and slimy amphibians.

I spend a lot of time in nature, but smells really get to me. The worst was when Mom and I walked into Longburger Funeral Home. Trixie's parents greeted us at the front door like they were welcoming us into their home. I guess they kind of were, since they own the place. I remember their sympathetic faces and clammy hands.

But that smell. I'll remember that smell forever.

It's hard to describe the death smell in words, but you recognize it right away, and then it stays with you.

In the science classroom Mr. Dover weaves through lab tables, peering over shoulders. He's wearing a light blue bow tie covered in flies. We have to complete the frog dissection with our symposium partner because Mr. Dover says, "It's a way to build camaraderie."

I'm staying on top of things and watching Mouton closely. There's nothing scarier than Mouton with a scalpel. He can paint and all, but I don't fully trust him with a blade.

I wipe the scalpel clean with a rag. "I'll take it from here, Mouton. Cover me, I'm going in."

"Sure thing," he mumbles. Then, as clear as can be, he says, "Eddie-shovel-truck!"

I pause before cutting the frog and look up at him. As badly as I want to say "Seriously, stop saying that," I know he can't control it, even though he might be trying his hardest.

I refocus on the frog and press the scalpel into the frog's abdomen. I make one horizontal incision and two vertical ones, and then I peel back the skin. Inside the frog is a cluster of dark-colored balls.

Mouton shoots his arms into the air, like we just won a contest. "Raisins! We found raisins!"

"They're babies. Not raisins," Mr. Dover says, standing behind us. "Your frog was going to have tadpoles.".

I can't decide which is worse, Mr. Dover standing behind me or the frog death smell. Or that Mouton thought our frog was going to have raisins.

Mr. Dover straightens his bow tie. "Eddie, that was a precise incision. Now finish removing the organs and complete the lab report with Mouton."

Mr. Dover moves on to Gabriela and Trixie's table. Gabriela handles the scalpel like a pro during the dissection process. She's calm and in control, like a surgeon.

Trixie is a different story. She watches from behind

Gabriela with a grossed-out look on her face, like the frog's going to come alive and jump on her head.

Mr. Dover watches them closely. "Gabriela, have you ever done a dissection before? You're very good at this."

Gabriela tucks a strand of hair behind her ear. "I helped at an animal shelter in Brazil. But those animals were alive."

"Very nice," Mr. Dover says. "Keep up the good work."

Mr. Dover moves on to the next table.

I clean the scalpel, wrap it up inside a paper towel, and place it on the metal tray next to the other dissection tools.

Gabriela and Trixie move back to their desks to work on their lab reports.

Mouton leans over our frog, examining the eggs.

I sneak over to Gabriela's dissection table to check out their frog. Mr. Dover was so impressed with Gabriela's incisions, but I want to judge them for myself.

Their frog's organs are spread out over their table. There's the liver, spleen, stomach, pancreas.

And that's when the death smell hits me. Between the dead frogs, the cleaning solutions on each table, and the freshly waxed tile floors in the classroom, the odor is the same as the funeral home.

The smell makes me think of Dad lying in the casket, dressed in his favorite birding outfit, his binoculars tucked beside him, his hands resting at his side.

But it's not just about Dad anymore.

In my mind I see Mr. Dover holding the tiny slip of paper from the robin's nest and saying, "Mouton." I picture Gabriela and Chase sitting in the booth at the Freeze Queen. I imagine the winners of the science symposium standing on the big stage, holding shiny blue ribbons, and I'm not one of them.

My stomach can't take everything at once.

I swallow twice to keep from getting sick, but it doesn't help. I cover my mouth and run out of the classroom.

Moving On

After science class I get sick in the hallway at my locker, and again in the cafeteria after sitting down with my lunch tray and a chicken patty special.

One look at the chicken patty sandwich, and I lose it.

At least Mom is there to comfort me. It's a little embarrassing when Mom rubs my head and says "It's okay, sweetie," but I don't mind it. I feel terrible, and when you feel like that, there's nothing more comforting than your own mom.

I spend the rest of the day in the nurse's office.

Mom says I'm too young to spend the day alone at home, so I have to wait until she gets off work.

After the last bell rings, Mom decides to skip working late and she drives me straight home. During the drive she says, "I'm sorry about Gabriela. Just remember, she's new in town, she can use all the friends she can get."

"She hates me."

"Listen, Eddie. I'm sure Gabriela doesn't hate you. She was just meeting someone new. You can't be mad at her for making new friends."

"It's not just about Gabriela. It's everything." I look out the window, watching the mailboxes go by in a blur.

Mom reaches over and pats my leg, letting me know she's there for me. Usually I'd pull away from her and tell her to stop, but this time I don't.

Every half hour or so at home, Mom checks on me. The bubbly feeling in my stomach is gone, but now my mouth is dry and my tongue feels like sandpaper.

Mom knocks on my bedroom door and comes in, carrying a glass of ice water. "We're out of orange juice."

I sit up in bed. "That's okay."

"Take small sips. It'll make you feel better."

Mom sits on my bed, close to me, like she wants to talk. "So why'd you get sick in the first place? Did you eat an old Buck Burger from your locker?" She laughs at herself, coughing twice, her keys jingling to the same rhythm.

"There was this smell in the science room. It smelled like the funeral home, and then I started thinking about Dad. Next thing I know, I'm thinking about everything else that's going wrong. I just couldn't take it anymore."

Mom's expression turns serious. She puts her hand on my cheek. "Oh, Eddie," she says, her eyes becoming watery. "I'm sorry."

I put my hand on top of hers. "It's not your fault, Mom. Like Dad told us, 'We have to keep on living, keep moving on.'"

Mom squeezes my hand. I squeeze hers.

"You know," she says, "your dad looked forward to you having Mr. Dover as a teacher."

I pull my hand away from hers. "What? Dad said that?"

Mom shifts on the bed. "Despite what your dad told you about Mr. Dover, he knows a lot about science, especially birds. Dad knew you would be in good hands."

"Well, Dad wouldn't think that way if he knew Mr. Dover put me with Mouton on purpose."

"Are you sure he did it on purpose?"

"I mean, I'm not one hundred percent sure, but it seems that way."

Mom rests her hand on my knee. "Maybe Mr. Dover knew you and Mouton would make a good team. Maybe he thought Mouton needed you."

I take a sip of water. Mouton and I are far from a good team. We're not even a team, more like a pair of mismatched socks.

Mom messes up my hair. Then she gets up from the bed. "Get some rest," she says. She walks out of my room, closing the door behind her.

I take a sip of water and think about everything Dad said about Mr. Dover. According to Mom, Dad thought Mr. Dover was an okay guy. And if that's right, then Dad wasn't telling me the whole truth about Mr. Dover.

I set the glass of water on the table next to my bed. I pull the covers to my chin and close my eyes, hoping this is all a bad dream.

One Piercing
Eye

The next morning I open my eyes before the sun comes up. My stomach feels better, so I get out of bed and get dressed. The science symposium is next week, so I want to spend as much time as possible at Miss Dorothy's place. The only way to prove my hypothesis—that a golden eagle can be found in West Plains—is to take a photo of it.

When I walk into the kitchen, Mom is standing at the sink. "You're supposed to be in bed," she says. She takes a drink of black coffee. Then she puffs from her cigarette and blows smoke out the cracked window.

"I'm fine," I tell her.

I open the fridge, but then I remember we're out of orange juice. I grab a granola bar and shove it into my pocket. Then I put on my jacket. "I'm going to Miss Dorothy's."

Mom blows smoke at the window. It spirals into a mini tornado and slips outside between the window and the sill.

"Can I borrow your camera?" I ask her.

"What for?"

"In case I see the golden eagle."

"Go ahead. It's on my dresser."

Before getting the camera from Mom's room, I stand there and watch her take another puff from her cigarette. "I really wish you'd quit smoking."

Mom puts the cigarette down in the ashtray. She looks at me for a long time.

Finally, instead of inhaling again, she turns on the faucet and holds the cigarette underneath the running water. The cigarette sizzles, its glow disappearing.

I smile.

Mom smiles.

Before I walk out of the kitchen she says, "Good luck!"

I'm sure Mom isn't going to quit smoking just like that. But she listened to me, and that's a start.

Soar

* * *

When I step outside, the cool morning air greets me. I pedal toward Miss Dorothy's, my breath rolling out in tiny bursts.

I walk my bike through the side yard.

Miss Dorothy opens the back door and waves.

"Morning, Miss Dorothy!" I shout.

She reaches into a Dan's Sporting Goods plastic bag and tosses a handful of seed out the door. Before she can throw a second handful, a flock of northern bobwhites swoops down and starts pecking at the ground.

When I get to the pond, I take out my binoculars and look up at the squirrel tied to the tree. It looks the same as it did yesterday.

Coop hasn't touched it, and she might even be protecting it.

I steer my bike through the grass while Coop scares off some scavenging crows. She knows I need the squirrel.

I squat down and wait, my fingers crossed inside my coat pocket, hoping for a glimpse of the golden eagle.

Coop flaps twice and glides overhead.

"I knew I would find you here," a voice says from behind me.

I stand up and turn around.

Gabriela stands about ten feet away from me. Her hair is longer and shinier than ever, her eyes rounder and browner. She tucks her chin deep into a scarf wrapped around her neck. Her jacket looks too light to keep her warm. I'd offer her mine, but I'm not sure if we're still good enough friends for that.

"I've got work to do," I say.

"Eddie. We need to talk."

"There's nothing to talk about."

"I am sorry. I did not mean to hurt you. Your costume was the best part of the night. I had to tell someone about it, and Chase was there."

"He was there, all right."

"Chase and I are friends. Just like you and me. I am sorry if that makes you unhappy, but I am meeting new people every day. And this makes me feel like I belong here."

I bury my chin in my jacket, trying to stay warm. "You're right. I should be happy for you. You're just listening to the music."

"Yes, exactly. And you have made it easier for me."

"I have?"

"Of course. You are funny, interesting, courageous.

And most of all, you have real feelings and you are not afraid to show them."

"So you really like all that stuff about me?" I can't help but feel confused. Here I am trying to impress Gabriela, and the one thing she likes most about me is my most embarrassing moment when my feelings came out.

"More than anything else," she says. "A person who reveals his feelings is a person who knows himself. A person who knows himself is a person who can know others."

"Wow," I say. "That sounds deep."

"My father is a deep person. He also likes you very much."

I can't help but let a smile escape from the corner of my mouth.

Gabriela stares at the ground. She shoves her hands deep into her pockets, her breath coming out in small clouds.

"I'm glad we're friends," I say.

"Me too."

I reach down and pull a long, wispy piece of grass from near the pond. I tear it apart, one small section at a time, letting the pieces fall from my hand.

"I am sorry about your project, Eddie."

"What do you mean? My project is still going."

"But the eagle is not here."

"He'll be here. You just have to be patient. John Audubon sat and watched birds for hours, until every detail about the bird was burned into his mind forever. How do you think he made his paintings look so real?"

"But what if the eagle never comes, and then you cannot prove your hypothesis?"

"He'll come," I say.

"You keep saying 'him' and 'his.' How do you know this eagle is a male?"

"Dad told me so."

Coop flies overhead, like she's been listening to our conversation and she understands what I'm saying. She lands on a branch above us, spreads her wings, and stares at us. At least there's one bird cooperating with me. That's more than I can say about the golden eagle.

"Do you believe everything your dad told you?" Gabriela asks.

I tear off another piece of grass and throw it down. "Yes. I do."

Gabriela walks closer to me. She looks up into the tree at Coop, who still perches on the branch. "She is so beautiful."

"And loyal."

Coop opens her wings wide, like she's stretching to start her day, then goes back to her normal perching posture.

"Eddie," Gabriela says.

"Yeah?"

"Do you think your father was perfect?"

I look up into the tree, at Coop. I notice her broad shoulders. Her long, rounded tail. Her hooked beak. Her sharp talons. She's the ultimate raptor. And then I notice the one thing that sets her apart from the other hawks.

Her one piercing eye.

I wonder if Dad really thought that I'd be in good hands with Mr. Dover. And if so, why didn't he ever tell me?

"No one is perfect," I say. "But my dad was his own person. And that's good enough for me."

Golden Feather

Later in the week Mr. Dover lectures us about the cane toad taking over parts of Australia. I couldn't care less about the cane toad or anything else he has to say, so I spend the time sketching Coop in my journal.

Mr. Dover stops in mid-sentence. "Eddie?"

I look up from my journal. I close it quickly and decide I'd better pay attention, even if cane toads make me think of the death smell.

After school I stop by Miss Dorothy's to check on my traps and the squirrel tied up in the tree. I guide my

Soar

Predator around the property and notice a feather on the ground below one of the oak trees. It's long, narrow, and brown. I put down the kickstand on my bike and run toward it.

As I get closer, my heart starts beating so fast, it feels like it's coming through my shirt.

I pick up the feather and hold it. It's slender and soft. The base is white, and the top part is golden brown.

I recognize the kind of feather right away.

It's a golden eagle secondary wing feather!

I feel like dipping the feather in ink and writing "Blue Ribbon" across the sky. Instead I carefully place the feather inside my jacket pocket, close to my racing heart.

Then I take out my binoculars and look up at the squirrel tied up in the tree. Half the squirrel is gone!

I drop my binoculars, letting them dangle around my neck. I climb the tree and bag the remaining squirrel carcass. It's more evidence that a golden eagle was here. It's just what I need to prove my hypothesis. Now if only the golden eagle would reveal itself so I can snap a photo of it and document its appearance.

Coop flaps her wings twice and glides overhead. She lets out a loud *cak-cak-cak.*

"Thank you," I say to her. "You knew what I needed all along."

After I leave Miss Dorothy's place, I stop by Mouton's house to share the good news. I park my Predator in his driveway and rush to the front porch with the brown couch. Out of breath, I ring the doorbell, but the doorbell doesn't work. I knock on the screen door. It rattles back at me, like it's being bothered and telling me to go away.

Mouton finally comes to the door. His hair looks like an abandoned sparrow's nest. He's wearing a black T-shirt with a yellow smiley face on the front, and baggy jeans.

"What do you want, Eddie?"

"I just want to see the painting. Then I'll go home."

He runs his fingers through his hair. Then he opens and closes his mouth three times, like he's trying to make his ears pop.

"What are you talking about?" he says. "What painting?"

Golden
Failure

Mouton! You were supposed to paint the golden
eagle!" My pulse goes crazy, and I grab my
hair with both hands.

"I'm not painting anything for you. Yip-yip."

"But you agreed to do it! Here I am, busting my tail
working on everything else. And I found a golden eagle
feather today! Do you know what that means?"

Mouton opens the door and walks outside. It
doesn't seem to bother him that I'm about to pull out
my hair. He plops down on the brown couch. Dust
clouds rise from the cushions.

"I haven't felt like painting," he says, his shoulders slumping.

"But what about your voice? This is your chance to let everyone hear you loud and clear. This is your chance to say what you *want* to say."

Mouton looks up at me. "That's the problem. I don't *know* what I want to say."

"Okay, listen. We don't have time for pouting. We need to problem solve here. How long does it take to paint a golden eagle, to make it look good, like the one you painted of Coop?"

"About a week."

"What? We don't have a week! We have three days! The symposium is on Monday."

"It's art, Eddie. It takes time to make it right."

"I can't believe this! All this time I thought I could trust you." I pace back and forth on the front porch. Frustrated, I kick the brown couch, and more dust fills the air.

Mouton opens and closes his hands quickly. He makes a fist, then opens his hand, makes another fist, then opens. "Eddie-shovel-truck," he says.

He stares out at the street. His eyes look lost, in another place, another time. For a second I kind of feel bad for him. I realize that no one has ever listened to what he *wants* to say or do. Maybe if I stop telling Mouton what to do and give him a choice, he'll finally come around to doing what's right.

"Look, Mouton. If you don't want to paint the golden eagle, then there's nothing I can do about it. It's up to you."

Mouton puts his head down, his hands resting on his thighs. He stays that way for a long time.

He finally looks up. "Okay. I'll paint the bird. It might not be my best work, but I'll do it."

I look at him for a long time, like when Mom looked at me before she held her cigarette under the faucet. "Are you serious? You're really going to do it?"

He nods. "Yes. I want to."

I smile, because there's nothing else left to do. "I can't wait for everyone to see your work. You're going to be the talk of the town."

I jump off the front porch and walk toward my bike, my hands jammed into my coat pockets. My short breaths jump out in shapes the size of hummingbirds, and fly away, like they were never there to begin with.

While pedaling away from Mouton's house, I look behind me and wave.

Mouton sits on the couch, looking down at his hands, which keep opening and closing beyond his control.

During the weekend, I stay up late working on our project. I glue the typed portions of our research to our three-panel poster board. I center the title—"Finding Gold"—across the top and then place the other elements on the board in strategic places.

On the left panel of the poster board, I place the purpose and hypothesis. In the middle, below the title, I put the materials list. On the right side I glue the evidence and conclusion.

I gather the materials to display on our table at the symposium. It's always good to have objects to show the judges. It takes your project to the blue-ribbon level.

On my desk I place the spool of string, my binoculars, Dad's night vision binoculars, the cross pouch, a granola bar, and the golden eagle feather. I'm also taking my bike to stand next to our table, because that's how I made it back and forth between my house and Miss Dorothy's place.

By the end of the night, everything is in place except

Soar

Mouton's painting. If he comes through and finishes the painting, we'll have a chance at the blue ribbon.

If he doesn't, we'll be remembered as a mismatched pair of socks—with holes in them.

The Big Day

The science symposium is the biggest event in West Plains for seventh graders.

Sixth graders like to check out what they'll be doing next year. Eighth graders like to compare their projects to the current ones. Seventh graders—well, we're the stars of the big show!

I've been to every science symposium since I was born. Dad was one of the most well-known winners ever, so the school sent him an invitation every year. Dad couldn't wait to point out what he thought were the winning projects.

Three years ago, when I was in fourth grade, he

predicted the top three projects, from third to first place. That was the same year his body started to slow down.

This year a new sign, surrounded by balloons and streamers, hangs above the entrance to the gym.

WELCOME TO THE GREATEST SHOW IN SCIENCE!

Decorations cover the gym walls. There are giant posters of famous scientists, like Einstein, Salk, Newton, and Galileo. Cartoony-looking pictures of telescopes, beakers, and calculators fill in the gaps between the scientists. More balloons stream from the basketball hoops.

Everyone, including me, is busy setting up their booths, making them look good for the judges. Mr. Dover and Mrs. Hughes are two of the judges, but the third judge won't be revealed until right before the symposium begins.

The gym is divided into two sections, with a giant blue curtain hanging in the middle. The parents and special visitors sit on one side of the curtain, while Mr. Dover introduces himself and babbles on about the symposium's history. On the other side, hidden from all the visitors, we stand at our tables, ready to explain our projects to whoever wants to listen.

The key is to impress the judges, so you have to be prepared when they come knocking.

Our booth has come together perfectly. The poster board stands in the middle of the table, with a sheet hanging over it and birding gear spread all around it. On the table sits my cross pouch, flashlight, granola bar (because energy leads to alertness, and alertness leads to spotting birds), and Dad's night vision binoculars. There's also the missing link—the golden eagle feather.

In front of the table stands my Predator, resting on its shiny kickstand.

Everything on the outside looks great. On the inside I'm a little nervous about what the judges will think of my findings.

Unless the golden eagle comes flying through the gym doors and perches in the rafters, my hypothesis will remain unproven. I never officially saw the golden eagle, so I have no photo or documentation to prove it was in West Plains. But I do have the feather I found at Miss Dorothy's place, which might be enough physical evidence to impress the judges.

That doesn't mean my project is a failure. It just means my project has to stand out even more than the others. I'm counting on my birding expertise and thorough scientific explanation to keep me in the running for the blue ribbon. Students have won before without proving their hypothesis. It can be done.

Gabriela's booth is across the gym, near the curtain. She places things carefully on the table and then steps back to make sure they're exactly where she wants them. She, too, has her poster board covered with a sheet.

She and Trixie have kept their project a secret since Mr. Dover assigned it, and while I pretend not to care, I really want to know what their project is about.

Over the next several minutes the gym becomes as busy as a train station.

Seventh graders hustle around, perfecting their displays. Other seventh-grade teachers, who are there to help, walk through the booths, making sure that every group has what they need.

On the other side of the curtain, the crowd becomes louder. I can't see who's over there, but the gym must be filling up with parents and grandparents and everyone else in town who wants to see the symposium projects.

Mr. Dover, wearing a navy-blue blazer, walks over to

my booth. He straightens his bow tie, which is bright red and covered with white symbols from the periodic table of elements. On one side of his tie is "Fe" for Iron and "He" for Helium.

"I'm eager to see your project," he says.

"Yeah, well, my partner's nowhere to be found."

I look around the gym for Mouton, but I don't see him anywhere. Up until this point, I wondered if Mouton actually finished the painting. But now I'm getting worried that he won't show up at all!

Mr. Dover checks his watch. "No need to panic yet. He still has fifteen minutes."

"What if Mouton doesn't show up? Can I still win the blue ribbon?"

"I don't know," he says. "That's never happened before. I would have to confer with the other judges."

"You mean, you'd actually consider not penalizing me?"

"Well, I'm not sure about that. Remember, no matter what happens, you're still judged on how well you and Mouton worked together. After all, this is a *group* project."

In that case, our project is doomed . . . unless I find Mouton.

Searching for Mouton

I suddenly don't feel so well. I look around for any signs of Mouton. I don't see him, so I take a step toward the gym doors to go look in the hallway.

But then I see Chase walking up to Gabriela's booth, and I stop. My first thought is, *He's an eighth grader. What's he doing here?* Then I notice that he's holding a roll of electrical tape, which means he got out of class to help prepare for the event. I'm sure he volunteered just so he could see Gabriela.

Chase tosses the roll of tape in the air and catches it behind his back. He says something to Gabriela, and she laughs and smiles at him.

Then Gabriela turns and sees me watching her.

I look away, and move the binoculars closer to the granola bar, and the granola bar closer to the cross pouch, but my act doesn't work.

When I glance up, Gabriela is walking toward me.

"Good luck, Eddie," she says.

"Thanks. I'll need it."

"Where is Mouton?"

"I don't know. Have you seen him anywhere?" I fidget with Dad's night vision binoculars on the table, deciding whether to stand them upright or lay them down. I decide to display them upright because it makes them look more important.

Gabriela adjusts the shoulder strap on her dress. "I thought you and Mouton had everything figured out."

"We do. I mean, we did. It turned out different than I expected, but I guess that's part of the scientific process. Kind of like order and progress."

"Good memory," she says.

Chase walks up, tossing the electrical tape in the air again and again. He's a full head taller than me, and his arms are the size of my thighs. "Nice display, Eddie."

"Thanks."

I can't figure out why he's calling me Eddie. He's never called me by my real name.

Chase rubs his chin like Dad used to after shaving. "Good luck, man. Hope you win the blue ribbon."

Gabriela punches Chase in the shoulder.

"Ouch," he says. "Actually, I hope you get second place." He walks away, tossing the tape roll into the air, catching it between his elbows.

"What was that all about?" I ask Gabriela.

"Chase is a nice person. He is not as bad as you think."

"I think he's just acting that way to impress you."

She rolls her eyes. "If it is not one thing, it is another. And if you really want to know, I did not tell Chase to be nice to you. That was his own choice."

"Oh yeah, prove it."

"After you left the Freeze Queen, I told him more about you, and then he felt bad about how he talked to you."

"What'd you tell him about me?"

"I told him that you know everything about birds, that you are really sweet, and that you are my best friend."

I look down at my feet. No one has ever called me

a best friend before, not even Camilla. When I look up at Gabriela, a cool sensation, like the refreshing feeling from Papa's berry drink, spreads through my body. "It's been a long time since I've had a best friend."

"Ruby and Eagle," she says.

She smiles and walks away, back to her booth, where she begins rearranging items on her table.

Before I can think about best friends, Mom jingles my way, a spray bottle hooked onto her belt loop, a greasy rag jammed into her pocket.

"Hey, sweetie." She puts her arm around me. "Let's see this project of yours."

"Mom, you're supposed to be in the audience. The symposium is about to begin."

"What's your bike doing here?" she asks. She takes the handlebars and leans my bike away from her to get a better look at it. "Now, that's one sparkling frame."

"It's part of our project," I tell her.

"Speaking of your project, where's your trusty teammate?"

"He's not here yet." I look around the gym, then at my watch. "If he doesn't show up, I'm going to—"

"Now, now, Eddie. Remember, Mouton is a little unpredictable. We both know that."

"Tell me about it."

"Well, listen. You stay here and tidy up your presentation. I'll look for Mouton in the hallway, just to make sure he's not lost. If I find him, I'll tell him to report to base immediately."

"Thanks, Mom, but you don't have to do that."

"I know I don't have to. I *want* to." Mom kisses my forehead and says, "Knock 'em dead, champ."

She walks away, her keys clinking together on her hip. She stops in the middle of the gym, bends down, and wipes away a scuff mark on the wood floor. Sometimes she just can't help but clean up after people.

Science
Symposium Saga

At three o'clock sharp Mr. Dover's voice blares over the speakers from the other side of the curtain. He introduces himself and then rambles on about the very first science symposium and how it began an honored tradition at West Plains Middle School.

After his speech the curtain opens, and all the people move toward us. It's a sea of endless heads and bodies, old and young.

A crowd goes to Gabriela's booth first. Papa stands in the front.

Once everyone settles down, Gabriela pulls off the sheet and reveals her display board. Everyone steps closer to their table, blocking my view. There are some *oohs* and *ahhs* and even a few claps. Trixie stands to the side of their table, smiling, her orange braces reflecting the bright gym lights.

All I can see is the title running along the top of their display board: "Bird Talkers."

I should've known that's what their project is about. Gabriela had access to the perfect subjects. Her research was taking place in her own backyard. Literally.

Most of the crowd is stuck at the first few booths, so I leave the sheet draped over our poster board. It's important to reveal your project in front of a big crowd. Drama creates buzz, and buzz catches the judges' attention.

But I have a bigger issue right now. Mouton. He's still not—

"I'm here!"

I turn to the voice, and Mouton rushes toward me! He holds a square-shaped object with a red-and-white striped beach towel hanging over it.

"Where have you been?"

Mouton catches his breath. He wipes his forehead with his shirt. "I was finishing the painting, just like I promised."

"Seriously?" I try not to make a scene in front of everyone. "You finished it?"

"Yip!"

"Yes! Mouton! You came through!"

I try to give him a high five and a chest bump, like the basketball players do when they score a basket, but he just stands there.

The crowd pushes toward our booth. In about twenty seconds they'll hound us and we'll be under the microscope. We have to be ready for the big reveal, or we'll miss our only opportunity to create blue-ribbon buzz.

"Hurry. Set the painting on the easel," I tell him.

But then I take the painting from Mouton and do the work myself. He'd never get it facing the right way, at the right blue-ribbon-winning angle. "Okay. Here's the plan. Are you listening?"

Mouton turns pale. He doesn't have much color to begin with, so this makes him look almost see-through. "I'm listening. Yip!"

"When everyone gets to our booth, you just stand there and smile. Don't say anything, don't touch anything."

"Just stand here and smile," he repeats. He shifts

his weight from one leg to the other, like he's swaying back and forth to music only he can hear.

"Stay calm," I tell him. "Everything is in order now."

"Yip!"

"I'm going to introduce our project and then pull the sheet off the poster board. When I do that, you pull the towel off your painting. It's the moment we've been waiting for. Got it?"

"Eddie-shovel-truck!" he says.

"Does that mean 'yes'?"

He nods.

The crowd from Gabriela's booth begins moving toward us.

"Quick, get in place," I tell Mouton.

The crowd closes in fast. People begin forming a half circle around our table, waiting for us to impress them with our project.

Mr. Dover and Mrs. Hughes hold clipboards. They both wear JUDGE badges on lanyards around their necks.

Mom pushes her way to the front of the crowd. She gives me a thumbs-up, her keys on her belt loop clinking together.

Then I notice another familiar face in the crowd.

Sandy.

He leans in close, scanning our poster board. When he sees my Predator, he gives me a thumbs-up. And then I notice that he's also holding a clipboard, and a JUDGE badge hangs around *his* neck too!

I almost scream and dance and shout to the sky.

SANDY IS A JUDGE!

Sandy knows me better than anyone else. Dad was his favorite person. He fixed my Predator, and he loves birds. He's the best judge I could ask for!

But then I realize there's another side to Sandy being a judge. If I win the blue ribbon, everyone will say I had an unfair advantage. Mr. Dover will put one of those funny-looking stars next to my name in the blue-ribbon record book, and the integrity of my project will be questioned forever.

Now that I think about it, Sandy being a judge has made things really complicated. I'll definitely need his vote to win, so there's only one thing to do—impress him until his toothless smile fills the gym and he picks us as the winners.

Mouton must be nervous, because he keeps saying "Yip-yip" under his breath, but I can tell he's trying to control his vocal tics. I don't even care, because this is Mouton's time to shine. It's time for everyone to hear his voice—through his artwork—loud and clear.

Mom shushes the crowd around our table. Everyone begins to quiet down. That's when I know it's time for me to start my presentation. So I clear my throat and begin talking.

"The eagle is a symbol of power and integrity, honor and freedom, the fight to not only survive but to dominate. The golden eagle is the most efficient hunter on the planet, and it has only been seen once before in our town . . . until now."

I pull off the sheet, revealing our poster board.

Everyone gasps.

Mom gives me another thumbs-up.

Sandy leans in closer, inspecting my research. He begins writing notes on his clipboard.

Mr. Dover straightens his bow tie.

Mrs. Hughes begins taking notes, looking up, down, up, down.

I take the feather carefully off the table and hold it up. "The truth is, the golden eagle lives right here, in our own backyard. How do I know this for sure? Before I was born, my dad saw one at Miss Dorothy's place. Its wingspan was two meters long and its talons were the size of bear claws. As you'll see in my conclusion, I've found evidence that the golden eagle has returned to West Plains. You might call it a theory. I call it . . . the truth."

I nod at Mouton.

"Yip-yip!" he says.

He yanks the red-and-white striped beach towel off the painting.

The crowd gasps, only this time it sounds like the air seeping out of a bike tire.

The painting is NOT a golden eagle.

It's the painting of the two boys in the sandbox, one holding a shovel, the other holding a toy truck.

Mouton takes the painting off the easel, holds it up high, and shouts, "Eddie-shovel-truck! Eddie-shovel-truck! Eddie-shovel-truck!"

My mouth hangs open.

The golden eagle feather drops from my hand and sinks to the gym floor.

Leaving It
All Behind

Silence fills the area around my table. It actually feels like the whole gym is silent. Most of the faces I can see are expressionless and looking at Mouton's painting. Some people are even laughing.

I become so mad that my eyes fill with tears.

I decide to walk away from it all.

I hurry toward the green neon exit sign, stepping on the golden eagle feather. Brushing past Mom, I cut through the crowd, leaving behind my hopes of a blue ribbon. Leaving behind Mouton, who's still holding up his stupid painting.

"Eddie!" Mom calls after me.

I keep walking. And I'm not stopping.

When I get to the exit, I slam through the double doors and find myself in the hallway that connects the gym to the rest of the school. I walk quickly down the hallway. I don't know where I'm going, but I've got to keep moving until I get out of this place.

My bottom lip begins to shake, and my eyes fill with more tears. Everything around me turns blurry and out of focus. *I will not cry*, I tell myself. *I will not cry*.

This isn't really happening. It's all a dream. Some stupid dream with a stupid painting at some stupid science symposium. I'll wake up soon, and it'll be the day of the real science symposium, the one I'm going to win.

Behind me I hear my mom burst through the double doors. She calls after me. "Eddie! Come back here! Eddie!"

I keep walking, my heart beating faster, my vision more blurred.

Mom runs down the hallway after me, her squeaky footsteps on the tile floor getting closer with each step I take.

She finally catches up with me, outside of Mr. Dover's classroom, of all places. She grabs me by the shoulders, spinning me around.

"Eddie," she says, out of breath. "I'm sorry, sweetie. I'm so sorry."

"He ruined everything!" I tell her, my bottom lip trembling. "I tried to be nice to him. I tried to help him, and he ruined it! I hate him!"

"Sweetie, I know it's bad, but you can't just walk out like this. You have to go back and finish what you started."

"It *is* finished. Everything is finished!"

"It doesn't have to be. What about all the effort you put into this project? There's a lot to be said for that."

"No one cares about my effort. They're all looking at Mouton's stupid painting."

"That's not your problem, Eddie."

"It is too my problem, when he's my one and only partner and he screws everything up. Now we have no chance of winning the blue ribbon."

Mom takes me by the shoulders and stands me up straight. She looks me in the eye. "What would your dad say right now? Just think about that. What would he tell you to do in this situation?"

I take a deep breath. Another one. I will not cry.

Mom holds a look on me. "He'd tell you to get your butt in there and stand tall, to be proud of your work.

He'd tell you to focus on controlling your own actions, not Mouton's. It's not your fault that Mouton brought the wrong painting. "

I nod, agreeing with her, even though I don't want to.

"Well, guess what?" she says. "Your dad isn't here anymore. He's gone, forever. I'm sorry, sweetie, but that's the truth and you need to hear it. But I'm here, Eddie. It's me and you, you and me. And I'm telling you to be strong and carry on, just like you said about us."

"What about the blue ribbon?"

"Eddie, who cares about the blue ribbon? That doesn't make or break your project. It's about the process, not the result."

I think about that for a moment. It doesn't sound like something Mom would say. "Who told you that?" I ask her.

"Who do you think?"

I stand up straighter, taller, my shoulders back. I inhale deeply to clear my head and push back my tears. "Dad?"

"Yes, Eddie. He told me that."

"When?"

"You really wanna know?"

I nod.

Mom looks down at the floor. She takes out her cleaning rag and wipes a black smudge away from the tile, her keys jingling against her leg. She stands up, stuffing the rag into her back pocket.

"Our marriage wasn't always the best," she says, still looking at the floor. "We were going through a rough patch after you were born. I wanted to leave, and your dad stopped me."

"You wanted to leave Dad? Like, take me away from him?"

"I had my suitcase packed. I was leaving, Eddie. I mean, I was out of here."

Mom crosses her arms over her chest to keep herself from getting upset. "Then your dad told me that being married was about the process of companionship. He said that we should focus more on the moment and enjoy being together, and not worry so much about our future."

"Then what happened?"

"We got better, and you grew up."

Mom laughs one of those little laughs that keeps you from crying. I think this one keeps us both from crying.

I look down at the spot on the floor that she wiped

clean. I can't believe she almost left Dad forever. If that had happened, I would've never known about the food chain or the Rules of Birding. I would've never learned how to identify birds by their voices.

I would've never known about Sandy and Dad's friendship.

I would've never known about the golden eagle.

Mom smiles at me, resting her hands on my shoulders. "Now come on. I bet there's a line of curious people in there waiting to ask you questions about that bird."

I take a deep breath, because it's the only way I know how to respond; it's the only way to keep from losing it and running away from this place.

Mom puts her arm around me, and we walk toward the entrance to the gym.

Blue-Ribbon Winner

When I come back into the gym, Mom walks me to my table. But the big crowd has moved on to other tables. There are only two people checking out our project. One is reading our poster board, and the other is looking at the golden eagle feather.

I look around the gym, but I can't find Mouton anywhere.

Holding his clipboard, Mr. Dover walks up to us. "Eddie, I'm sorry about what happened. Mouton's mother took him home for the day."

"Good. I don't ever want to see him again."

"Eddie." Mom nudges me with her elbow.

"Well, I can't promise you won't see him again," Mr. Dover says. "But I think it's best that he's not here for the remainder of the symposium."

"Thanks, Mr. Dover," Mom says. "Eddie and I talked about what happened. He'll be fine."

"Yeah," I say. "Just fine."

I make it through the rest of the symposium in one piece. I'm able to keep my emotions together enough to answer questions and to show off my project. But I can't stop thinking about the stunned faces in the crowd when Mouton yanked the towel away and revealed the stupidest painting ever.

At four o'clock everyone gathers around the stage, waiting for the awards ceremony to begin.

Mom is the only person standing next to me, probably because no one else knows what to say to me.

When I think about Mouton and the painting, my fists clench. He's lucky that he left early, or there would've been a fight right here on the gym floor. I've never been in a fight. The only thing I've ever punched is Dad's shoulder. But there's a first time for everything, including fist-fighting symposium partners.

I'm not sure if Mouton meant to bring that painting

or if he accidentally brought the wrong one. Right now it doesn't matter. He did it, and there's no turning back time.

I wouldn't be so mad if Mouton cared about the symposium, or cared about anything other than woodpecker pens. He's probably at home laughing right now, while my blue-ribbon dreams were shot down and wrangled by the neck, like the quail at Miss Dorothy's place.

On the stage, Mr. Dover steps up to the microphone, holding his clipboard. "Okay, everyone, if I could have your attention, please. It's time to announce the winners of this year's science symposium."

Mom puts her arm around me. She knows this is going to be hard for both of us to hear. As much as I want to pull away from her, because it's kind of embarrassing to have your mom's arm draped on your shoulder at a school event, I need her arm around me right now more than ever.

Mr. Dover says, "In third place, Josh and Jacob Simmons."

Everyone in the crowd claps. One section of the crowd erupts into cheers and whistles. Must be their family.

The two boys come up onstage, and Mr. Dover hands them each a small plaque.

It's no surprise they got third place. The Simmons boys are identical twins, and they're identically good scientists. Their project was about how to make a hybrid airplane. I'm not sure it's really possible, because their theory was based mostly on putting solar panels on the wings to help charge the engines. I guess it would save fuel costs for airlines, but only on sunny days.

Mr. Dover leans into the microphone. "In second place, Mandy Russell and Sophia Everton."

Again everyone claps. The two girls rush up to the stage, smiling and giggling, while camera flashes go off in every direction. Their project tested the effects of home aquariums on families' blood pressure. They hypothesized that families with aquariums in their homes would have lower blood pressure than those without aquariums, and their research proved that they were right.

Mom begins rubbing my back. I can only look at the stage in disappointment, knowing that my name will not be called.

Mr. Dover hands the girls their plaques, and they move to the side of the stage.

"And the winners of this year's science symposium are"—Mr. Dover looks down at his list one more time— "Gabriela Oliveira and Trixie Longburger."

Soar

The crowd cheers loudly. Gabriela and Trixie walk up to the stage, all smiles.

I don't know what to think.

On one hand, it's now official that I didn't even finish in the top three. On the other hand, Gabriela and Trixie won the blue ribbon!

Mr. Dover hands each of them a giant blue ribbon. The top part of the ribbon is shaped like a medallion with gold lettering and two long streamers flowing from it. Under the stage lights the ribbons shine like rare pieces of gold.

Mom keeps her arm around me. She even tightens her grip.

I clap once, because it's hard to be happy for someone else right now. It's even hard to be happy for Gabriela.

Mr. Dover's Truth

I've spent the last two days in bed playing sick. Mom knows I'm not sick, but she feels sorry for me, so she let me stay home. She knows how much the symposium meant to me and how it'll be impossible to show my face—or any part of me—at school. If it were up to me, I'd stay in bed for the rest of the year.

Mom opens the door to my room and comes in, carrying a glass of orange juice. She sets the glass on the nightstand. "Just what the doctor ordered."

"Thanks, Mom." I take the glass and gulp down half of the orange juice.

"You know, you can't stay in bed for the rest of your life. Tomorrow it's back to school."

"But, Mom—"

She rests her hand on my arm. "Listen, I know you're disappointed about the symposium. But just like you said about us, you have to move on. Besides, two sick days for you means two sick days for me. I only get so many of them."

I collapse against the pillows. How can I go back to school after being humiliated at the event I wanted to win more than anything else?

"Also, we have plans on Saturday, so make yourself available." Mom kisses my forehead and walks out of my room, shutting the door.

I wonder what plans she could be talking about. Maybe she's taking me somewhere special, somewhere far away, like to one of those fancy birding tours where everyone tips the guide because they see so many rare species.

I wonder if they ever see golden eagles.

For the rest of the day, I lie in bed, staring at the ceiling. I think about that quote Dad used to say all the time and how it relates to what happened at the symposium.

"But Hopes are Shy Birds flying at a great distance seldom reached by the best of Guns."

My HOPES of winning the blue ribbon vanished when Mouton brought the wrong painting.

The golden eagle is a SHY BIRD, and I'll never see it.

And then there's Mr. Dover and his hunting GUNS. I'm sure he's at home celebrating because I didn't win the blue ribbon.

The next morning I find Gabriela at the bus stop. Her breath twirls out in small clouds and disappears into the cool air.

I stop about ten feet away from her and say "Congrats," the way I rehearsed it fifty times in front of the bathroom mirror.

"I am sorry about what happened," she says. "You are right. Mouton is a jerk."

"It was a mistake. We all make them. He just made it at the worst time ever."

"You are not mad at Mouton?"

"I was mad for a while. But it's over now, and there's nothing I can do about it. I guess it's time to move on."

"Eddie, thank you for saying 'congrats.' That was sweet of you."

I give her a half smile.

And at that moment—even though it's getting colder outside and I can see my breath—my body becomes a little warmer on the inside.

Mouton doesn't show up at school, which is a good thing, because I'm not ready to see him yet. I'll see him at some point, and when that happens, I'm not sure how I'll react.

After science class Mr. Dover asks me to stay behind and talk to him.

On her way out Gabriela walks past me. "Do not let Mr. Dover make mountains out of mole hills."

She touches my shoulder, and I feel like I could fly. I never thought having a best friend could make me feel that way.

When everyone is gone, I stop by Mr. Dover's desk.

Mr. Dover stands up, straightening his bow tie. It's purple, with yellow question marks on it. He hops up onto the front table and sits there, his legs dangling free. "You know why I wear this bow tie with question marks on it?"

I wasn't really prepared for a question about his bow tie. "Uh, no."

"Because it has to do with what happened at the symposium."

"It does?"

"I wear it because science, just like real life, is full of unexplainable conclusions. Eddie, no one knows why Mouton brought that painting to the symposium. We may *never* know why he did it. Maybe Mouton can't even answer that."

"The reason doesn't matter. It's over now."

"Very mature of you, Eddie. But it wasn't Mouton's fault that you didn't win the symposium. After what happened, we decided to judge your project solely on the research. If I'm being honest with you, it was because of Sandy. He didn't think your field study was thorough enough. He thought you should have conducted research in other locations, besides Miss Dorothy's place."

"Sandy?" I say out loud. I feel like I've been stabbed in the back by the sharp bill of a great blue heron.

"Eddie, your scientific methods were impressive. You're a natural ornithologist. In fact, Mrs. Hughes and I talked about your project for a long time. But Sandy felt your research was limited geographically. After we added up the scores, you came in just off the podium."

I shrug, trying to make it seem like no big deal.

How could Sandy do this to me? He's supposed to be on *my* team.

Instead of asking Mr. Dover more questions about the symposium, I remember Mom telling me about how the process is more important than the result. Maybe she was right.

"You know," I say. "I had this whole idea of winning the blue ribbon, just like my dad, and that idea became more important to me than my actual project. But then I realized that winning the blue ribbon isn't the only important part. It's about the process of getting there. I guess I lost sight of that."

When I finish saying it, I'm not sure if I believe myself.

Mr. Dover smiles. "That is the most insightful thing I've heard from any student this year, Eddie. You're definitely growing into yourself."

"Thanks," I say.

The bird clock on the back wall chirps.

I take off my backpack and unzip it. "Before I leave, I have something to show you."

I reach inside and pull out the beige envelope that was taped to Dad's symposium poster. I hold out the envelope to Mr. Dover. "I found this in my garage."

Mr. Dover takes the envelope, slides his finger

across the seal, and opens it. He looks inside and pulls out the newspaper article. He holds it in front of him, staring at it, reading it.

I finally speak up. "Is this why you don't like me?"

Mr. Dover keeps his eyes on the newspaper article. He sighs. "Your father and I were actually good friends in seventh grade. We discussed our symposium projects, and even offered to help one another."

"If you were such good friends, then what happened?"

Mr. Dover slides the newspaper article back inside the envelope. "We began forming our own opinions. We both loved science and birding, but we always approached our passions differently. I was more 'by the book,' and your father was—how should I say this—'creatively ingenious.'"

"So that's it? You were just two different people?"

"Well, that's not exactly the whole story."

"Then what *really* happened?"

"After the symposium your father was unapologetic about winning, and I selfishly wanted his blue ribbon. We began to go our separate ways. And then we both entered a statewide birding competition. That was officially the end of our friendship."

Mr. Dover offers the beige envelope to me.

I take the envelope and hold it in both hands. "Who won the competition?"

Mr. Dover looks down, then at me. "Neither of us," he says. "We were so focused on beating each other that we forgot about everyone else."

I hold the envelope, waiting for Mr. Dover to say something else, but he doesn't. Finally I walk away.

Then I stop at the classroom door.

I turn and look at Mr. Dover and everything surrounding him.

The periodic table of elements poster on the far wall, just like the Brazilian flag at Gabriela's house.

The beakers and test tubes in the tall cabinet, next to Mr. Dover's desk.

The lab tables in the back of the room.

The bird clock on the back wall.

The green markers that Mr. Dover always uses.

Mr. Dover's rolled-up sleeves.

His bow tie, full of question marks.

Then I remember how Mr. Dover brought Zeus, the American kestrel, to school.

I wonder if he brought Zeus because he had to keep a close eye on his injured wing, or if he brought him for me. I'm pretty sure he brought him for me.

"Mr. Dover?"

Mr. Dover looks up, his legs still dangling from the front table.

"Will you say 'hi' to Zeus for me?"

Mr. Dover nods. "I'll do that, Eddie."

"Thanks," I say.

I turn and leave the classroom.

While walking down the hallway, I think about what Dad said about Mr. Dover being a good teacher, and me being in good hands.

I think I'm starting to agree with him.

Birthday Surprise

When I wake up on Saturday morning, colorful balloons cover the backyard. Two fold-up tables and a bunch of chairs fill the screened-in porch. If that's not enough, Mom has hung a giant number thirteen on the back door.

"Mom? What's all this about?"

"It's for your birthday party. Surprise!"

"Really, Mom?"

"Oh, don't worry," she says. "I only invited a few people."

I go to my room and sit at my desk. I open my bird journal and look at my drawing of Zeus. It makes me think about Mr. Dover and everything he said about my dad. I guess he's right—all friendships don't last forever. But I wonder if best friends have a better chance of surviving, and what that means for Gabriela and me.

There's a knock on my bedroom door. Mom opens the door. "Eddie, your first birthday guest is here."

"Who is it?"

"Sandy," she says, before blowing up another balloon.

"Mom! You invited Sandy?"

"We made up at the symposium. Hugged and everything."

I never told Mom about Sandy's opinion of my project. I don't want Mom to be mad at him again, so my only option is to confront him myself.

I walk outside to the back porch and find Sandy hovering over the table of food.

He turns to me and holds out a small package wrapped in newspaper. "I thought you should have this. It's not much."

I take the package and pull apart the newspaper, uncovering a blue ribbon. It's a medallion shape, with two long streamers, just like the blue ribbon Gabriela won.

"It's the blue ribbon I won in seventh grade. I want you to have it."

"I can't take this." I try handing it back to him.

Sandy nudges my hand away. "Lamb Dover called me last night. He told me about your conversation and what you said about losing sight of the process. You're going to make one heck of an ornithologist, Eddie. But you're an even better person."

I run my finger along the blue ribbon's outer circle, and then over the gold lettering that says "First Place."

Sandy takes the blue ribbon from me and pins it to my shirt. He smiles his toothless smile and pushes up his hat. "A perfect fit."

Having Sandy's blue ribbon makes me feel better about my symposium project. But what he says about me becoming "one heck of an ornithologist" fills me with pride I've never felt before. "Thanks, Sandy."

Sandy offers his hand, and we shake. While shaking my hand, he touches my shoulder and smiles.

After I drink two cups of orange juice, Gabriela and Papa come through the back gate.

Gabriela walks up and hugs me. "Happy Birthday, Eddie." She looks at the blue ribbon pinned to my shirt.

"It was Sandy's. He wanted me to have it."

"It looks natural," she says.

Silvio perches on Papa's shoulder. Papa signs something to Silvio, and Silvio says, "Happy Birthday! Happy Birthday!"

We all laugh at Silvio, and Papa laughs too.

Next, Miss Dorothy hobbles through the gate with a flock of quail trailing behind her. She throws seed on the ground, and they keep pecking at it.

"My Eddie," she says. "Happy Birthday." She rubs my hair, like Mom usually does, and hobbles over to the food table, which is piled high with Buck Burgers.

Soon Mom brings out the cake and everyone circles around me and sings "Happy Birthday." Mom leads the singing, and everyone is off-key, but it's okay with me. I pretend everyone is a goldfinch and singing, *Po-ta-to-chip, po-ta-to-chip, po-ta-to-chip.*

Right as I'm about to blow out the candles, the back gate opens and slams shut. I look up, the heat from the candles warming my chin.

It's Mouton.

Becoming Partners

Mouton holds up what looks like a painting, with the red-and-white striped beach towel covering it. He looks like he's holding in a smile and can't let it out.

I want to run up and punch him in the face.

But instead I control my emotions while glaring at him. First he ruins our project. Now he's trying to crash my birthday party. I've given him enough chances. I'm not letting him get away with this.

Before I can say anything, he yanks the towel away from the painting.

We all stand motionless on the screened-in porch.

The candles on the cake burn brightly.

I straighten up all the way, looking closely at the painting.

It's a golden eagle!

I scoot around the table to take a closer look.

The golden eagle looks real, like it's alive.

Gleaming gold feathers shine from its head and neck. Long wings extend from its body, which is covered in a golden sheen. Its powerful beak points downward, ready to tear flesh from bone. The eye that you can see in the painting offers a deep and piercing stare.

"Eddie," Mom orders. "Blow out the candles."

I turn around and lean down toward the birthday cake. I take in a deep breath and blow out the candles. Then I walk toward Mouton. The closer I get, the more perfect and more real the golden eagle looks.

"You're not welcome here, Mouton. So get out." I point at the gate.

"I saw your bird," he says. "Yip."

It takes a few seconds for his words to process in my mind. I blink hard, making sure I heard him right. "Wait a second. You saw the golden eagle?"

Mouton lowers the painting and holds it in front of him. "Yip!"

"I don't believe you."

"It's true, so believe it. Eddie-shovel-truck."

"When did you see it last? Where did you see it?" I can't get out my questions fast enough.

"After the symposium. At my house."

"Have you seen it since then?"

"No," he says.

My heart beats faster, and I begin pacing back and forth. "Okay, okay, stay calm," I tell myself.

Mom comes over to me. "Eddie, are you okay?"

Still pacing. "Yeah, I'm fine. I just need a minute to think about whether this is actually possible. I mean, if it's possible Mouton saw the golden eagle."

I think about the time of year. Late October. I recall Mouton's backyard, even though I saw it in the dark. Full of tall trees with large branches. Perfect landing spots for golden eagles.

"Here." Mouton offers the painting to me.

I stop pacing and look at him.

"This is for you. For your birthday. I'm sorry about the symposium. Yip."

I take the painting from him and hold it, looking it over. The only thing I can remember coming close to this is a golden eagle photograph in one of Dad's *National*

Geographic magazines. I want to reach out and stroke the bird's head, but then I realize I'd be touching paint, not a real bird.

Mom leans over my shoulder. "That is some bird," she whispers.

I turn to her, holding out the painting. "Take it."

"Eddie? It's yours. I'm not taking it. Mouton gave it to you."

"I know, I know. I mean, can you take it inside and put it in my room? But be careful carrying it through the house. I have to go find this bird."

Mom looks at me. She's not happy.

"Please, Mom?"

"Eddie, you can't leave your own birthday party. I'm about to cut the cake. You haven't even opened presents yet."

"I'll wash dishes for a month. Two months. A year!"

"Eddie?" She holds a look on me, a look that tells me I'm making a bad decision and she's not agreeing with me.

"But, Mom, this could be my only chance. Mouton saw the golden eagle."

Mom leans in close to me. "You don't know if he's telling the truth. Do you really trust him after what happened at the symposium?"

Soar

I look back at everyone gathered around my birth-day cake. Papa is showing Miss Dorothy and Sandy how to pet Silvio. Everyone came here for me, and now I want to leave them. Maybe Mom has a point. What if Mouton isn't telling the truth?

Then I see Gabriela. She mouths something to me that looks like "Go!"

I turn to Mouton. "Mouton, look at me."

I grab on to his broad shoulders and hold on to them, just like Mom did to me in the hallway outside the gym. "Look me in the eye and tell me the truth. Did you really see the golden eagle?"

Mouton's eyes are big and blue. I've never noticed how blue. He tenses up and says "Yip-yip!" like twenty times without stopping.

"Mouton, answer me. Come on, you can do it."

He looks at me, frozen in time and space. Then he speaks. "It was so big. It was like a flying dinosaur! Yip! I thought it was going to pick me up and carry me away! It had a spot on its wing."

I look at the painting in Mom's hands. I lean in close, looking at the golden eagle's wing. Then I find the gray spot, right there on the primary feathers.

I turn to Mom. "He's telling the truth. I have to go."

Mom looks back at Papa and Miss Dorothy and Gabriela and Sandy. Now they're all watching us, and I wonder how long they've been listening.

Then Mom reaches into her back pocket and shoves her camera at me. "Fine. But I want proof."

I take the camera and hug her. "Thanks, Mom."

Then I look at Mouton. "Come on! We have a bird to find."

Finding Gold

Mouton and I carry the brown couch from his front porch to his backyard. We flip the couch over and crouch behind it.

I take out my binoculars and scan the sky. It's midafternoon, and there's still plenty of daylight left.

"Thanks for the painting. I know exactly where I'm hanging it."

Mouton only says, "Yip."

"I thought it took you a long time to paint something that good."

"Usually it does. But when I saw the golden eagle, everything came out faster. *A lot* faster."

"Take a look." I hand him the binoculars. "Maybe you'll have better luck."

He takes the binoculars and moves them too quickly across the sky, so I tell him to slow down and I show him how to do it properly.

An hour later we share a bag of potato chips and try chewing without making any noise. Then we sit in silence for a while and listen to the songbirds in the trees. I tell Mouton the name of the bird that's singing, and every time, he says, "How do you know that?"

And every time, I say, "It's in my blood."

After another hour and still no golden eagle, I hold up the binoculars and look from east to west. Then I finally work up the courage to confront Mouton. "So tell me, what happened at the symposium?"

"What?" he asks, staring at the sky.

"Out of all your paintings, why did you bring that one?"

"Because it was the only one that fit."

"Fit what?"

"The symposium. You and me. Eddie and Mouton. Shovel and truck. Yip."

It hits me all at once, like being slapped in the back with a science book. I lower the binoculars and look at Mouton.

"Eddie. Shovel. Truck," I say slowly.

I remember Mom saying that Mouton and I used to play at the park in the sandbox together. We built sand castles and dug tunnels and . . . played with shovels and trucks.

"The painting is us," I say, thinking out loud. "We're the two boys in the sandbox."

Mouton nods, and I know I'm right. "I brought the painting because I want Eddie back."

"What do you mean?"

"I want to be friends again, like before we were in kindergarten. Yip."

I stare at the ground.

All these years of fighting with Mouton meant he just wanted to play in the sandbox and go back to the way things were. I don't know what to feel besides guilty and responsible for everything he did to me.

"When we started kindergarten, you stopped playing with me," he says. "You only cared about birds."

"I'm sorry. I didn't mean to ignore you."

He shrugs. "I'm sorry about your bike. I guess it was my way of getting revenge. I was mad at you and didn't know how to handle it. I feel bad about messing it up."

"That's okay," I tell him. "Sandy fixed it. I'm just glad you showed up at my party and told me about the golden eagle."

Mouton looks at me. "Eddie-shovel-truck. Eddie-shovel-truck." He can't control it.

Then I say, "Mouton-shovel-truck."

We both laugh under our breath, and then we end up laughing harder and harder until my stomach hurts. The funniest part is that we're trying to laugh quietly since we're on an important birding trip and we shouldn't be making any noise at all.

But that only makes us laugh more.

While laughing, I roll onto my back, looking up at the sky, holding my stomach, my breath rolling out into the cold afternoon air. Then I notice a dark speck against the clear blue sky.

The speck is a bird. It starts out small, but I can tell it's a lot bigger than an American crow or a brown-headed cowbird.

I grab the binoculars off the ground and scan the sky. It takes me a second to find the bird and focus on it.

The bird's wings are lifted in a V-shape, its feathers spread like fingers.

As it gets closer, the sunlight shines off the golden

glow on the back of its head. And then it tucks its huge talons underneath its body. Its sharp call fills the sky, and that's when I know I'm not dreaming.

I keep my eyes inside the binoculars and reach out and touch Mouton's arm. I don't say anything, just touch him and hope that he's seeing the same thing as me.

"Here." I hand him the binoculars.

I pull out Mom's camera, point it to the sky, and click, click, click away until I'm sure I have enough proof.

The golden eagle flies closer to us and swoops down, and for a moment we're caught in its shadow, which spreads over us and covers the whole couch. It circles above the backyard, showing off its massive wings, including the one with a gray spot on it.

I stare past the bird, into the bright sky, and see a glimmer of light.

Maybe it's a reflection, or a star that's come out early. Maybe I'm imagining the light and it's not really there.

Or maybe it's Dad—yeah, Dad—and he's looking down on me.

He reaches down—all the way down from above the clouds—and puts his hand on my shoulder.

I look up at him.

Tracy Edward Wymer

I see his smile.

I breathe in his woodsy smell.

I hear his words.

"That's my boy," he says.

And the golden eagle—*our* golden eagle—spreads its wings and soars higher, disappearing into the never-ending sky.

Eddie's Bird Log

Commons

American crow

American goldfinch

American robin

Carolina chickadee

eastern bluebird

house finch

house sparrow

mourning dove

Betters

blue jay

brown-headed cowbird

downy woodpecker

great blue heron

indigo bunting

northern bobwhite

northern cardinal

northern flicker

northern mockingbird

red-bellied woodpecker

red-headed woodpecker

ruby-throated hummingbird

Raptors

American kestrel

bald eagle

barred owl

black vulture

Cooper's hawk

eastern screech-owl

golden eagle

great horned owl

peregrine falcon

red-tailed hawk

sharp-shinned hawk

Rare Species

great green macaw

hyacinth macaw

scarlet macaw

More about Birds

The Cornell Lab of Ornithology—All About Birds
allaboutbirds.org

National Geographic—Birds
animals.nationalgeographic.com/animals/birds

American Birding Association—Young Birders
youngbirders.aba.org

National Audubon Society
audubon.org

World Parrot Trust
parrots.org

The ARA Project—Saving Macaws
thearaproject.org

Cheer, cheer, cheer!

(This means 'thank you' in bird talk.)

Writing is very much a solitary art form, but in reality it takes an entire flock to give a book its wings.

I'd first like to thank my awesome agent John Rudolph and my amazing editor Alyson Heller. You both championed Eddie from the beginning, and without that enthusiasm and support, the world would have one less book.

I'd also like to thank the following birds; you all helped this story take flight:

The entire team at Aladdin! You rock the book world!

Brian Biggs—for creating the perfect cover for this story.

Elizabeth Kuelbs, Tina Christopulos, Dee Garretson— for being the best critique partners ever, and for never tiring of Eddie and his golden eagle.

Claudia Antoine—for hiring me all those years ago and changing the course of my writing life.

Cherie Boss—for introducing me to birds and their unique personalities, and for being a wonderful friend and colleague.

Craig Didden (Mr. Dover)—for wearing bow ties and being a real-life bird nerd.

Barbara Williams—for your breadth of bird knowledge, and for your expertise and guidance.

Evelyn Skye—for reading early on, and for pushing me to become a better writer.

Mike Winchell—for being an entire support system in just one person! You are a fine friend and tenacious storyteller.

Paul Murphy—for your useful feedback on early versions of this story, and for your humorous take on everything in the world.

Mr. Dicken—for introducing me to Shakespeare, and for letting me read my poems in front of the whole class, even when my writings were slightly inappropriate.

Teacher-Librarians—for your support, for always talking books, and for embracing my stories. You have the most important jobs in the world.

Linda Sue Park—for teaching me how to write scene by scene, and for being a mentor and inspiration on the long road to publishing a book.

Diane—for putting up with me when I talk too much about birds.

Mason and Logan—for always being excited for daddy's new books, and for reading them (or pretending to read them).

Mom and Dad—for always being proud of my accomplishments, big or small.

Looking for another great book?
Find it
IN THE MIDDLE.

Fun, fantastic books for kids
in the in-be**TWEEN** age.

IntheMiddleBooks.com

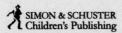 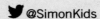

Did you LOVE reading this book?

Visit the Whyville...

Where you can:

- ◯ Discover great books!
- ◯ Meet new friends!
- ◯ Read exclusive sneak peeks and more!

Log on to visit now!
bookhive.whyville.net